# Gun Feud

A tall man, clad in dusty range-garb, the wide brim of a
flat-crowned Stetson shading a lean, sweat-streaked face,
rode into town. Slung low at his flat hips, thonged down
with rawhide strips, were two Colt .45s. This was Will
Callender, fearless and furious and after revenge.

He had come out of Arizona to seek his brother's
killers and make trouble for a lawless bunch. Nothing and
nobody was going to stand in his way. This, then, is the
gripping story of Callender's bullet-bitten vengeance
trail. A red-blooded, fast-paced yarn indeed.

# Gun Feud

## FRANK ARNSIDE

**A Black Horse Western**

ROBERT HALE · LONDON

ISBN 0 7090 6930 8

Robert Hale Limited
Clerkenwell House
Clerkenwell Green
London EC1R 0HT

Typeset by
Derek Doyle & Associates, Liverpool.
Printed and bound in Great Britain by
Antony Rowe Limited, Wiltshire

# ONE

Noon at Crimson Peak, New Mexico.

The wide ribbon of the town's single street scorched in the blaze of the high sun. Three horses stood hitched at the rack outside Whit's store, switching their tails at the annoying flies. From under the sun-blasted awnings shading the plank-walks sharp-eyed loafers watched the solitary stranger who came riding at a walk on a weary palomino.

He rode with the easy slouch of a man used to long hours in saddle leather, heading for the heat-warped clapboard structure of Rittendon's livery stable. He was a tall man, clad in dusty range-garb, the wide brim of a flat-crowned Stetson shading a lean, sweat-streaked face. Slung low at his flat hips, thonged down with rawhide strips, were two Colt .45s.

The powdery dust, stirred up by the hooves of the stranger's mount, rose in small plumes to drift into his back-trail on the slight, hot breeze that blew in from the desert flats.

To the idling loafers of Crimson Peak the rider had all the markings of a species of gun-packing humanity too familiar in this border country – the owlhoot drifter, on the dodge from the law in some other section of the frontier, who lived by his six-guns. To some of the watchers the tall stranger had a vaguely familiar appearance.

He swung down from the palomino's saddle at the wide doorway of Rittendon's livery. Seth Rittendon, squat, bald-headed and wearing a leather apron, come bowlegging out of the stable to stop in his tracks when he caught sight of his customer.

The liveryman, too, found this big gun-packer familiar. He stood for an instant taking in the bronzed features under the droop of the hat brim. The grey eyes with premature creases, caused by long squinting into the South-Western sun, splaying around them; the aquiline nose; the mouth that was tightly set without being the cruel mouth of a lobo trigger man and the general air of being no man's man but his own all reminded Seth Rittendon of another man.

The stranger, who was aged about thirty-five, fisted the reins into Rittendon's hand.

'Rub him down, feed and water him,' he said.

'Sure,' nodded the liveryman.

The big newcomer jerked his head towards a grimy eating-house on the far boardwalk. 'Is the grub in that place fit to eat?'

'You have to like it or leave it, friend, that's the only beanery in this burg,' the liveryman replied.

The stranger fixed Seth Rittendon with a keen stare, as though assessing whether or not he was of a friendly disposition, then he said levelly:

'Where's the best place to find Cy Tambaugh?'

Seth Rittendon felt a brief chilliness grip his innards. He eyed the big man's guns, worn so obviously in gunslinger fashion.

'Why, as it happens, he's in the Palacio Hotel right now.' Rittendon nodded towards a peeling wooden structure of two storeys standing next to Whit's store on the opposite side of the street to the eating-house. 'I can't rightly say whether Mister Tambaugh is hirin' any hands out at his CT spread right now, though,' added Rittendon.

'I didn't say I was lookin' for a job, did I?' rejoined the gun-hung stranger. 'However, my business with Tambaugh can wait a little till I eat.'

The liveryman felt the chill grip his innards again as he watched the big man angle off across the street with ringing spurs. At the eating-house labelled 'KURDIA'S CAFÉ' in sun-blistered paint, he pushed open a creaky door and entered.

The eating-house was as grimy inside as it was outside. A couple of rickety tables and a few chairs made up its inventory of furniture, apart from a long counter standing to one side. Behind this, with her back to the tall newcomer, worked a woman in a grubby smock, with jet-black hair hanging in unruly straggles down her back. The woman was the only person in the eating-joint, the atmosphere of which was dominated by the odour of stale food.

The big man sighed. Another border beanery with another slatternly woman slinging the hash!

He leaned his bulk against the counter. The woman turned and asked:

'What can I do for you?'

The stranger suppressed a gasp at the sight of the girl's face – for the back view of her in the soiled, shapeless overall had disguised the fact that she was only a girl. The big stranger felt a pang of shame at having tagged her for just another frowsy hash-slinger. The girl was about twenty-three, with an oval face and large blue eyes. There was a world of sadness in her eyes, a pallor on her cheeks and her raven hair was untidy but, even so, the girl was beautiful. She was slightly built and her voice was oddly cultured for this New Mexican desert rat-hole.

'Steak, potatoes, bread and coffee, ma'am,' ordered the man. The 'ma-am' was almost a reflex action, born of the average cowboy's respect for womenfolk. Had he only half an eye, this gun-hung stranger would have recognized the girl as a cut above the average eating-house counterhand and completely out of place in that capacity.

'I'll have it ready in just a few minutes,' she said, returning to the kerosene stove behind the counter on which a couple of pans steamed. The big stranger had not failed to notice the look that flitted across her face when he addressed her so respectfully. Nor did he fail to catch sight of her dainty but work-reddened hands. Whoever ran this greasy beanery, her parents, perhaps, obviously kept her hard at it and it was evident that she was used to scant respect from the customers.

While the big man was waiting for his order, a door at the rear of the counter opened and a small, middle-aged man whose sour face was as wrinkled as a sun-punished old Texas saddle came bowlegging in with a distinct limp. He was dressed in a countrified version of Eastern clothes, his eyes were small and his mouth hard. Paying no attention to the customer, he rapped:

'Stella, gimme a cup of coffee, pronto! You know I got business across the street in five minutes!'

The girl moved away as though well used to being completely subservient to this crabby little man.

'Hurry, girl,' nagged the man. 'Dammit, why must you move like you were all the time in a dream?' He still paid no attention to the customer in the café.

The tall stranger was leaning on the counter lazily, regarding the smaller man with smouldering eyes. He suddenly tipped back his Stetson and drawled:

'Eighteen hundred an' sixty-three!'

The middle-aged man started and stared at the café's customer, apparently seeing him for the first time. From his position behind the counter he could see only the upper part of the man's body. The ominous, thonged-down Colts were out of view.

'What'd you say?' he inquired.

'I said eighteen hundred an' sixty-three,' answered the stranger. 'That was the year President

Lincoln declared slavery to be illegal. From that year on it's been wrong for anyone in our country to treat another human creature as a slave. Unless New Mexico seceded from the Union without it comin' to my notice, I figure the no slavery law holds good here and, figurin' from the way you're addressin' this young lady, I guess maybe you should be reminded of the law!'

The smaller man looked thoroughly taken aback for an instant, then he took a step nearer the stranger and faced him across the stained counter. He shoved his leathery face very close to that of the customer. The set of his ugly gash of a mouth told the big newcomer to Crimson Peak that this was a crafty little *hombre*, not to be underestimated.

'Listen, mister,' growled Leathery Face, 'I own this joint an' I talk to my niece how I please. I don't take to saddle-tramps walkin' in here an' tryin' to teach me anythin'!'

The big man quirked his lips in a smile, but no humour was reflected in the steel-grey eyes. He acted suddenly, snapping out of his lazy, leaning posture and grabbing the café proprietor by the shoulders. The smaller man wriggled frantically, but the stranger hoisted him over the counter as easily as if he were a child, setting him down on his own side of the counter.

'If you were a younger man without a game leg, *hombre*, I'd drag you to the street by the tailboard of your britches an' I'd shove your face in the dirt,' rumbled the tall man.

The café proprietor wriggled free of the other's grip, staring with bugged eyes at the Colts in their tied-down holsters. His seamed face was ashen. For the first time he saw that this man wore the mark of the gunfighter – and he had called him a saddle-tramp. Never, in a life that had not been uneventful, had Jake Kurdia been so scared as he was at this moment.

He was quaking visibly as he made hastily for the street door. The stranger was leaning languidly against the counter again, smiling sardonically.

'What about the coffee you were in such an all-fired hurry for?'

'It can wait,' replied the jittery Kurdia. 'I have business with Mister Tambaugh!'

As the café owner opened the door, the man at the counter called:

'Tell him not to be in too big a hurry to leave town, 'cause Will Callender is comin' across the street to see him when he gets round to it, but first he's havin' himself a meal. You can tell Tambaugh that Will Callender figures he takes second place to a meal!'

Jake Kurdia stood chalk-faced on the threshold.

'Callender!' he husked. 'I knew there was some-thin' familiar about you!' Then he was gone, slam-ming the sun-warped door behind him. Through the grimy window of the café, Will Callender saw him making for the Palacio Hotel as fast as his game leg would allow.

The girl stood there motionless, watching Will

Callender over the counter. Callender shuffled uncomfortably when he realized that tears were brimming in her wide, sad eyes.

'Thank you,' she said simply.

'For what?' asked Will Callender.

'For standing up for me and for not hurting Uncle Jake. No one ever said anything to him for pushing me around before, but I thought you might go too far. I thought, you being—' She broke off, lost for words, but her fearful glance at the low-holstered Colts spoke for her.

Callender gave a resigned nod. 'You thought, me bein' a gunnie an' a Callender, I'd pull iron on your ignorant ole relative.'

'I didn't say that,' protested the girl, her strained face flushing slightly.

'You meant it and I can't blame you. I guess I wear the gunslick's brand pretty obviously an' I guess folks in these parts associate gunplay with the Callender name, but they're a long ways from the truth.'

The raven-haired girl had turned her back on him and was continuing the preparation of his meal. Will stood with his face turned to the dusty window, watching the entrance to the Palacio Hotel across the street. He had seen the limping café proprietor scuttle inside and there had been no activity from that quarter since the batwings had ceased swinging behind him.

'Did you know my brother, Bob, Miss—?'

'Rivers – Stella Rivers,' replied the girl. 'Yes, I

knew him.' She spoke quietly, avoiding the frank grey eyes of the tall stranger.

'Would you say he was a bank-robber and a killer?'

'It's hard to say he was—' faltered Stella Rivers. 'It's hard to think he could do such a thing. He was so quiet and hard working and – nice—'

'Yeah. Robbin' and killin' was not in his line,' agreed Will.

'But the fact remains he robbed the Crimson Peak Cattleman's Bank and killed the teller, Henry Dirks,' the girl said.

'That's what they say he did, Miss Rivers,' answered Will, a chill edge to his voice. 'They also say he made a one-man stand at his cabin on Silica Ridge and got shot to ribbons by the posse. He was innocent of that crime, ma'am. He was innocent as a new-born infant!'

'I'd like to think he was, too,' murmured the girl, 'But I can't forget I saw him galloping past this café in broad daylight after the robbery!'

'Did you see his face?' asked Will Callender eagerly.

'No, but I knew his clothing and his horse. There was a kerchief around the lower half of his face.'

Will glanced across at the Palacio again. A tall figure in black with a yellow brocaded waistcoat, a parsonical flat-crowned hat and a marshal's star gleaming from his breast, had stepped out of the hotel doorway and stood staring in the direction of the eating-house. A big Peacemaker Colt, buckled at the lawman's hip, was disclosed for a brief instant as an eddy of desert wind whipped back the skirt of his square-cut coat.

Will Callender knew the man on the porch of the Palacio. Without taking his eyes off him, he continued his conversation with the girl.

'Miss Rivers, I guess you knew my brother was an intelligent man. Maybe he was just another prospector to you folks in this neck of the woods, I guess he never told many people that he was a qualified mining engineer. To be a mining engineer a man needs brains and when a man with brains goes out to rob a bank he never goes in broad daylight on his well-known horse and wearing his usual clothing.'

'I never thought of it that way,' she said huskily as she placed Callender's meal on the counter.

Callender watched the man with the marshal's badge turn and re-enter the Palacio. The batwings pivoted in his back-trail and the range of vision afforded by the café window remained deserted. Will took his food to a table from which the street was still visible and began to eat, his eyes still on the Palacio Hotel across the street.

'A lot of people didn't seem to think of it that way, ma'am,' he told the girl. 'I don't know why I'm telling you this, but you say you liked Bob an' I'd like you to keep him in the right perspective. I know this is Tambaugh's town an' it's possible that you an' your uncle are Tambaugh folks, but I don't give a plugged nickel for Tambaugh, so I'll give you somethin' else to think over. From the talk I've heard around this territory, an' I've done a heap of investigatin' here an' there before I showed up in Crimson Peak, the posse that shot my brother dead in his cabin that afternoon three months ago was composed entirely of Cy Tambaugh's CT cowboys. What's more, Tambaugh worked a quick deal and got possession of the land my kid brother had owned in less than a month. A rich silver seam had been found by Bob, and Tambaugh's men are workin' it now!'

Stella Rivers nodded thoughtfully. Callender fell to eating in silence, still keeping an eye on the galleried front of the hotel across the street. The girl watched him with those large, unhappy eyes.

So strange a man, she thought. So much resembling a gun-hung border drifter at first glance, and yet so much more gentle than the average man of this rugged frontier. Never had she seen a man who bore the gunhawk stamp so boldly as this Will Callender, yet never had any man in this desert-edge settlement shown her the respect he had, or humiliated her blustering, bullying Uncle Jake as he had, on her account.

Stella's heart pounded at the thought that this man had come alone to make trouble for Cy Tambaugh. One man against Cy Tambaugh, cattle baron of the CT outfit, political overlord of this section of the territory; a ruthless, grasping, soulless man who owned this town and almost everyone in it. It was fantastic, she thought. Such a venture could only end one way – with Will Callender sprawled in the dust, a victim of Tambaugh's gunmen.

As he finished his meal Will asked the girl:

'What does your town marshal call himself?'

'Roy Collis,' she replied, noting the quirk that came to the lips of the tall man.

'I guess it goes without sayin' that he's Tambaugh's man, huh?' remarked Will as he paid for the meal.

'He's Tambaugh's man,' she answered, then added breathlessly: 'Be careful, Mr Callender. This is Tambaugh's town – it's madness to try to fight him alone!'

Will looked at the girl gravely for a long instant.

'We'll see about that,' he said.

She watched his mouth set into a hard line and he suddenly looked a different man – a hard man who would go after something and keep going, through hell and high water, until he got it.

He bid Stella Rivers "good afternoon" with a twitch of his hat brim and made for the door.

'Good luck!' murmured the girl hoarsely.

Through the grimy window pane she watched him walk across the hoof-pocked street until he disappeared behind the batwings of the Palacio.

# TWO

As he passed into the hotel, Will Callender knew full well that he might be walking into a gun-trap. The little café proprietor had been in the Palacio for twenty minutes or so and had had ample time to tell Cy Tambaugh of the gun-hung man who had announced his intention of going to the hotel. The black-garbed man sporting the star of a lawman, who Callender knew from another time and place, had stood on the gallery of the hotel, obviously on the lookout for Callender. Cy Tambaugh and whoever was with him inside had been given plenty of time to have guns trained on the door, awaiting the entrance of the tall stranger.

Callender knew he might be met by a withering hail of angry lead, but he was a man who knew human nature from long experience. All the advantages in this game were with Cy Tambaugh. Men of his calibre usually liked to play the cat for a while when they considered a mouse had fallen into their clutches. Callender felt the mighty Tambaugh would be unable to resist dangling the man who so boldly walked into his territory, loud-mouthing his intentions of bucking the Tambaugh faction, on a string for a little while. Tambaugh would, no doubt, like to snigger into the face of such a fool a few times before his hawks gunned him down.

Will was prepared to take a chance on this; nevertheless, his long fingers were splayed over the worn holsters at his hips as he shouldered open the batwings of the hotel.

There was no gunsong or slash of bullets as he entered. The vestibule of the hotel was dark after the white blaze of the sun out on the street. It was carpeted with a scuffed and worn carpet, long past its prime. A wooden staircase angled up at one side of the hall. Over to the right was a polished bar with fly-blown glass ornamentations and a sleepy-looking barkeep with a straggy moustache.

Seated on a worn, plush-upholstered seat that ran the length of the wall opposite the bar, drinks before them on a slop-stained table, were three men. The leathery-faced runt from the café was standing close to them.

All four had their eyes fixed on Will Callender as he walked towards them, spurs tinkling.

The middle one was Tambaugh. Will could hardly mistake his identity. He was paunchy, but would be tall when standing. He was clad in a pearl-grey suit and spotless linen shirt and was not wearing a gun. His face, adorned with a neatly-cultivated moustache, was flabby, but his nose was a craggy beak and his eyes were the flat, painted-on eyes of a killer. Cy Tambaugh was watching Callender with these hard eyes, his body shaking slightly with laughter that escaped his broad lips as a hissing titter.

On one side of him was the man in black with the marshal's star – the one who now called himself Roy Collis – on the other sat a youngster wearing a deputy marshal's star. He was wearing cowboy rig and had two Navy Colts buckled about his slim waist. Wisps of tawny hair escaped from under his greasy sombrero brim. Buck teeth protruded from his killer's mouth, and the eyes in his desert-bronzed features were those of a half-crazed hellion.

Will Callender walked slowly up to the seated trio and stood with legs apart before Cy Tambaugh. When he spoke his voice was gritty.

'My name is Will Callender and I've come to find the men who killed my brother, Bob. The individual members of the so-called posse can wait awhile. First, I want the truth about the whole set-up.'

Cy Tambaugh was still tittering at the man who had walked into his hands in this manner. Jake Kurdia was moving a little to one side, as though apprehensive of gunplay.

'Your brother was a bank-robber, *amigo*, and he was killed resisting arrest,' said Cy Tambaugh.

'Shut your mouth, Tambaugh,' hissed Callender. 'I'll do the talking. I know the man who robbed the bank in this town was not my brother. I know the whole business was a move of yours to grab the land on which Bob had recently struck it rich. I'm goin'' to prove it; I'm goin' to make you confess it with your own lips an' I'm goin' to finish you off.'

There was an uneasy twitch from the youngster with the deputy's star which Will did not miss with his gunslick's eye. Callender, with an eye trained to quick action, remained watching the still tittering Tambaugh, but was fully aware of the actions of the men seated on either side of him.

'See here,' began the man with the town marshal's badge, 'you can't walk in here and threaten—'

'Shut your face, Lafe Askew,' grated Will. He spoke in tones loaded with derision and did not even deign to look at the man he addressed. 'I don't care if they call you Marshal Roy Collis in this lousy town, you're Lafe Askew, of Arizona. I could gun you, throw your carcass over my horse, take it to Cochise County an' claim the hundred and fifty dollars' bounty Sheriff Behan has put on your bones. You don't know me, Askew, but I've seen you before an' I've looked at your face on plenty of reward dodgers. You're a back-shootin' rat. You killed one man in Tombstone an' two in Galeyville. In each case you shot them in the back. Don't talk to me, Askew, until I talk to you first. I don't converse with trash worth one hundred and fifty dollars dead or alive!'

The man in the black suit and brocaded waistcoat slumped back against the red plush of the seat, his jaw sagging, gasping as though he had been punched in the stomach. From the young, buck-toothed deputy came another nervous movement which Will watched with the tail of his eye.

Cy Tambaugh had stopped tittering.

Jake Kurdia had moved close to the bar and was making himself scarce.

Outside, one of the sun-punished and fly-tortured horses hitched at Whit's store gave a snorting whinny. There was a heavy silence until Will Callender spoke again. This time he addressed the youngster, facing him and looking squarely into his wild eyes.

'Don't try it, kid!' he warned. 'If you're out to make yourself a reputation, don't try to move up a rung by drawin' on me. It don't matter none to me if I have to spill your guts on the floor, but you might have a mother or a sister somewhere who'll grieve after you.'

The kid deputy's tow-coloured brows puckered down over his too-bright eyes. He made no reply, but simply glowered at Callender, who had turned his attention to Cy Tambaugh once more.

'As I was sayin', Tambaugh, I'm out to buck you an' every man-jack on your pay-roll until I get the truth about the deal you handed my kid brother.'

'You're a fool, Callender,' scorned Tambaugh. 'You're the biggest fool I've ever heard of!'

'Time will tell on that score,' retorted Callender.

Cy Tambaugh commenced to hiss out his wheezy titter once more.

'There ain't going to be much time left, Callender – for you, I mean!'

There was another, more decisive action from the kid deputy and Will Callender whirled with the speed of a panther to face him. The youngster was half standing, his Billy the Kid features twisted into a murderous mask and his hands clawed around the butts of half-drawn Colts.

The watchers saw Callender's hands streak down and upwards in a single eye-defying movement. His Colts cleared leather with an almost unbelievable rapidity before the youthful star-packer had fully drawn his weapons.

The youngster stood petrified for a moment and then went through with the draw. One of Callender's guns barked, stabbing out a red blade of flame. The youngster yelped like a kicked dog, dropped both his Navy Colts and clutched at his right arm. He fell back against Tambaugh on the seat, his mouth wide open and his eyes screwed up in a grimace of pain.

Through the drift of gunsmoke Will saw Tambaugh leaning forward across the table with eyes round as buttons. Marshal Collis, alias Lafe Askew, had placed both his hands on the table top, well away from the big Peacemaker bolstered at his belt. Callender knew there was no danger from that quarter. Askew was a back-shooter, drawing on a man to his face was not for him.

Will holstered his guns lazily.

'You were a fool, sonny,' he told the wounded deputy marshal. 'You should never have gone through with the draw when I had the drop on you.

Now, you've got a shattered arm – but that's better than havin' your mother or sister grievin' for you!'

'I'll kill you for this,' hissed the youth. 'I'll get you one day when you least expect it, *hombre*!'

Callender gave him a wolfish grin and nodded towards Askew.

'Don't fail to consult your boss on how to do it before you come gunnin', kid. He can give you plenty of advice on how to back-shoot a man. Follow his tutorin' real close an' you'll grow up to find that you too are valued at one hundred and fifty dollars by some sheriff. Must be a real comfort for a man to know what he's worth – 'specially when it's so damn' little that no bounty-hunter will bother comin' after him less he's plumb short of the price of a couple of drinks.'

'You're the fool around here, Callender,' gritted Cy Tambaugh. 'Like I just told you, you're the biggest fool I ever heard of. You'll never ride out of this country alive.'

Will Callender looked squarely at Tambaugh, hard points of light glowing in his grey eyes.

'You won't gun me down, Tambaugh,' his voice was flat and icy. 'None of your gunnies will come after me, either, an' I'll tell you why – I know Rosalind and I know where she is now!' He said the last part of the sentence with a slow deliberation, watching the effect of his words on the grey-clad cattle baron.

Cy Tambaugh turned pale. His jaw slackened and he half rose, clutching the edge of the table to support his heavy bulk.

'Rosalind!' he faltered in a hoarse whisper. 'What do you know about her? Where is she? Tell me!'

Callender laughed scornfully.

'When you tell me about Bob! I'll tell you about Rosalind when you come crawlin' after me ready to tell the truth about the way my brother was framed and butchered. I'll tell you all about Rosalind – before I kill you!'

The big man turned his back on the trio. Tambaugh was still standing there, ashen-faced, Collis–Askew was seated with his hands still clear of his gun, looking completely baffled by the trend the conversation between his boss and the big gun-packer had taken. The kid deputy sprawled on the seat holding his injured arm. Jake Kurdia and the barkeep were gingerly emerging from behind the bar, where they had ducked when the shooting commenced.

Walking slowly, Callender jangled his spurs in the direction of the door.

Cy Tambaugh called after him urgently and with a broken edge to his voice:

'Callender!'

Callender whirled about with that swift, gunslick's movement he had shown when turning on the kid deputy.

'Callender, I want to know about her!'

Will Callender hooked his thumbs into his cartridge-studded belt and spat disdainfully on the worn carpet.

'Like I said, Tambaugh – come crawlin'! I'll be around!'

Then he turned and strode through the batwings.

# THREE

One or two jittery faces stared from under the plank-walk awning and out of the doors of Crimson Peak's straggle of adobe and plank buildings. The sound of the shot slamming from the interior of the hotel had shaken the desert-edge town out of its early after-noon indolence.

Will Callender swung off the gallery of the Palacio. In doing so, he caught sight of the strained face of Stella Rivers watching him from the window of Kurdia's café.

He high-heeled his way to the tall wooden struc-ture of the livery barn. A wide-eyed Seth Rittendon saw him approaching and had Callender's El Paso saddle thrown over the palomino before the big man reached the high door of the stable. He named the price of the rub-down and feed as Callender took down his war-sack from behind his bedroll and checked it for provisions.

Rittendon took the payment without a word and

watched Callender mount and ride, wheeling the palomino to go out of town in the opposite direction to the way he had entered. When the tall rider had disappeared round the side of the livery barn, Seth Rittendon joined the excited townsfolk who were rushing across to the Palacio to see who had been shot. The stableman figured he was one up on the rest. After all, the gun-hung stranger had asked him where he could find Cy Tambaugh and curtly informed him he was not seeking the cattle baron to ask for a job at the CT outfit!

With this excitement broiling in his back-trail. Will rode easily in the direction of a hazy blue line of rugged country off to one side of the shimmering desert bottoms. Since his arrival in New Mexico from his home in Arizona he had spent a couple of days in sizing up this territory before ever entering Crimson Peak. Working with the cool precision he had employed in his man-hunting days in the Arizona Rangers, he had spotted the best section in which to make camp, for he had no intention of taking a room in the hostile town of Crimson Peak during his stay in this territory.

His move would be to make camp in a different part of the rugged, wooded ridge country each night. His knowledge of Rosalind was an insurance against Tambaugh personally trying to kill him in his sleep if he took a room at the Palacio, but there were others who might try – the wounded kid deputy, for instance. Possibly back-shooting Lafe Askew, who now called himself Roy Collis, might try it because

Will knew him for a cowardly Arizona owlhooter, but this was unlikely. The marshal of Crimson Peak, with his spotty reputation, was Tambaugh's man, and Tambaugh would not want Callender killed until he had learned what the big Arizonan knew of Rosalind.

Will rode thoughtfully under a sun that was a blazing white tyrant in the ultramarine sky, allowing the palomino to take the trail at its own pace. Presently he struck off up a coulee and was soon riding up the slant of a ridge studded with white oaks. The country here was of a greener character than the heat-hazed desert flats he could see below him to his left.

Another half-hour of steady riding brought him to a ridge-top from which he could see mile upon mile of purple-hazed wasteland on the one hand and a relief map of greener land, giving way to cattle ranges, on the other.

At his back, below him and looking like a cluster of toy houses from this distance, the town of Crimson Peak nestled at the edge of the wilderness. Up ahead he could see a small black square in the side of a craggy ridge. Men, made tiny by distance, moved about the black square. The black square was the mouth of a mineshaft and the men were Tambaugh's hirelings working the silver seam that had been discovered by young Bob Callender.

Two or three new shacks had sprung up around the mine as dwelling places for the men. The newness of their peeled logs told of their recent erection. An older shack stood to one side, looking somewhat lonesome. Callender, who had made a closer sortie of the country the previous day, figured that would be the cabin his prospecting brother had built, the one in which he had lived his hermit life and met his end at the hands of a so-called posse.

Callender halted his mount on the rim of the ridge for a moment, taking in the scene. Then he rode down the ridge to where a rocky declivity promised water and a camp site, leaving the scene at Silica Ridge to be swallowed by the blued distance.

To Will there had been a sudden temptation in that moment of looking down on Silica Ridge, temptation to unsheath the Winchester in his saddle scabbard and blast at the men around the mine workings. But that would have been a fool's move. The range was far too great for one thing and he had no idea whether any of the men down there had had a hand in Bob's death.

A tiny waterfall tinkled in the declivity and the place was sufficiently shaded and sheltered by white oaks and sun-split rocks to make a suitable site from which a campfire would scarcely be seen at a distance.

Will picketed his horse in a patch of sparse scrub which provided meagre grazing and unslung his saddle, war-sack and bedroll.

Building himself a cigarette, he squatted in the shade of a white oak, smoked for a while and reflected on the day's doings.

So far, so good. It was a pity about the trigger-happy kid deputy, but he'd asked for what he got and was lucky not to be served out with the certain death many another gunslinger would have given him when he followed through with his clumsy draw after being outdrawn.

Nevertheless, Callender would rather not have shattered the kid's arm, but the youngster had needed a lesson.

Callender considered his debut at Crimson Peak had got off to a good start. He had come to buck against Cy Tambaugh boldly and openly and he had done so in Tambaugh's own town and in front of his own men. He had done more. He had shown Tambaugh that he knew something of another side of the cattle baron's life and had effectively put an obstacle between Tambaugh and himself; an obstacle which would prevent Tambaugh from having him killed, at least until he had the information about Rosalind out of him.

Tambaugh wanted that information badly, as badly as Will wanted to avenge the murder of his kid brother and the ignominy that had been thrown on the youngster's name. But Callender was prepared to play a steady, waiting game.

*Poco a poco* – a little at a time – as the Mexicans said. A little at a time until Cy Tambaugh came crawling; a little at a time until Bob Callender's death was avenged.

Watching the upward drift of his tobacco smoke, Will fell to thinking of Stella. A nice name, he reflected, it meant 'star'; pity the stars that were her eyes were so grief-dimmed. He wondered what the girl's story was and why she was rustling beans in a greasy border eating-joint for the sour little runt she called her uncle.

Funny the way she had thanked him for putting the leathery-faced little cuss in his place and yet had been so grateful because Callender had not hurt him. Maybe she was genuinely fond of the little seed-wart.

There was no accounting for taste, Will decided.

Still, she was a mighty pretty girl. Pretty? Gosh darn it! She was beautiful and would be more so if some of that unhappiness was polished off her face with a smile!

Will tried to picture Stella Rivers wearing a fancy gown like those he had seen on Chicago women and with her hair dressed and braided. Then he snapped out of the daydream, telling himself he was an all-fired fool. He pitched away the butt of his ricepaper smoke and set to collecting oak branches and greasewood for a fire.

When the sharp chill of the desert evening hung on the air and long blue shadows were creeping around his camp site, Will had his fire lighted and a range-rider's coffee pot bubbling on the flames.

He was fishing a can of pork and beans from his war-sack when he heard the unmistakable sound of a hoof-clop on the nearby rocks.

Instinctively he dropped his war-sack and nudged his six-guns loose in their leather.

The hoof-tramp came nearer, but Will held his pose, squatting on his heels by the camp-fire as still as a frozen man, with a hand hovering close to a revolver butt.

Presently the form of an old horse surmounted by a big-hatted rider and a shapeless bundle of trappings came into view around the tumbled rocks at the edge of the declevity.

A hoarse voice hailed: 'Howdy, friend! I was passin' by when I catched sight of your camp-fire and figured I'd give you a neighbourly greetin'.'

At the sound of the unmusical, rasping tones, Will Callender sat bolt upright. In the firelight a look of disbelief took possession of his lean features, gradually melting into a grin.

The rider came into the compass of the firelight, which showed him to be a short man somewhere in his sixties. He wore cowboy garb which had seen much service. His right leg was missing from above the knee and replaced by a peg-leg which protruded stiffly outwards. The dancing flames of the fire illumined a seamed, broken-nosed face under the floppy brim of an ancient sombrero. The lower half of the newcomer's weathered mien was covered by an unkempt profusion of whiskers growing as wild as a prickly pear thicket.

'Figgered you might have a mouthful of cawfee fer a pilgrim,' grated the rider, 'so I decided to pay you a vis— doggone my ole hide! Will Callender!' He finished his sentence with a wild Rebel yell.

Will rose and strode across to the old-timer, extending an eager hand and grinning widely.

'Lone-Star Dobbins!' exclaimed the tall man. 'You

wall-eyed ole whiskey-guzzlin' son of a Texas scorpion! This can't be true!'

'Oh yes it is true,' grinned the oldster, swinging down from his scuffed Texas saddle. 'It's ole Lone-Star hisself, as much flabgasterated to see you as you are to clamp your honest eyes on me!'

The old cripple hobbled over to the fire and squatted on a rock. Will poured him a helping of fresh black coffee in his solitary tin cup, cut the top off the can of beans and pork and placed it on the fire to heat.

'What you doin' in this neck of nowhere, Will? Can't be Arizona Ranger duty this far into New Mexico – unless it's something special,' said the old man, sipping the coffee.

'Somethin' special, all right, but not Ranger duty – I resigned my commission a couple of weeks ago. First off, what are you doin' in these parts?'

'That's soon told,' snorted Lone-Star Dobbins disgustedly. 'I'm gettin' outta these parts, that's what I'm doin'.' He hooked a horny thumb towards the trappings on his overburdened old horse – a bundle of gunnysacks, a pick, a shovel and some battered placer pans. Been tryin' my hand at prospectin', but there's only the devil's own luck around here. I finished up near broke and got a job in a mine a little ways down yonder at a place called Silica Ridge. It's owned by a big *hombre* in these parts called Tambaugh an' ramrodded by a mean galoot named Chet Conners. I worked two days in the mine an' didn't like the place. There's somethin' funny about it an', what's more, I didn't like Conners, his way of doin' things or the majority of his crew. 'Bout an hour ago I told Conners to go to hell, collected my time an' rode out. I drifted into this hell-hole from Utah 'bout a month ago an' spent most of that time on the desert.'

Lone-Star paused while he accepted half the contents of the can of beans and pork which Will had spilled on to a tin platter.

'I hear tell there's a town called Crimson Peak down this way a piece an' I was aiming to get a couple of drinks there an' then head back to Arizona. I'd sooner be in jail in Tombstone than rich, drunk an' at liberty in this place!'

'Small wonder you didn't like the feel of that mine, Lone-Star,' said Will. 'My brother Bob hit that silver seam and was murdered for it about three months back. I was over Holbrook way on Ranger duty when I heard about it, so I resigned my commission then and there an' came gunnin'. As it happens, I've heard of Cy Tambaugh before an' I have somethin' on him from my days in Chicago that makes him plumb reluctant to kill me right now.'

Old Lone-Star listened wide-eyed as the big Arizonan told him the outline of the death of his brother and the crime he was supposed to have committed. He told the one-leggcd old Texan of his arrival in Crimson Peak and his meeting with Cy Tambaugh.

'By grab, Will,' exploded the old man. 'I never

knew there was a story like that behind the Silica Ridge mine. Come to think of it, a lot of those *hombres* workin' over there were obvious cowpokes an' could have been members of that posse you tell me was made up of CT riders. They were a tight-mouthed bunch all round. An' you tell me Lafe Askew is marshal of the town – the back-shootin' louse!'

'Yeah, but Lafe is small-fry. I believe he was the *hombre* who led the posse, but he's only a puppet dancin' on Tambaugh's string. I figure I can let him run awhile.'

The peg-legged Texan poured himself a second dash of coffee and began to chuckle hoarsely.

'Will,' he began in his gravel voice, 'meetin' up with you has provided just the opportunity I need to work off my ire. Fact is, I wasn't meant to be no prospector nor nothin' else but a fightin' man. I'm comin' in on this with you – it'll be just like the old Arizona Ranger days.'

'Now, look, Lone-Star,' protested Will Callender. 'This is a private fight. I came here to buck Tambaugh's outfit on my lonesome an' you don't have to stick your neck into any trouble on my account.'

The old-timer became suddenly serious.

'I owe you a favour, son,' he murmured, slapping the stump of his amputated leg. 'I ain't forgettin' what you did for me that time when we were two Arizona Rangers pinned down in the Dragoon Mountains by a bunch of murderin' thieves, an' me all shot to ribbons. It was the end of me as a Ranger, but you saved me from the gangrene an' maggots!'

Will fell silent, remembering the long, bullet-slashed days when he and his fellow Ranger had been penned in the Dragoons by terrible odds and the operation he had performed on Lone-Star's shattered leg with a bowie knife as his only instrument.

The old Texan produced his two heavy Colts from his belt and began to check the chambers.

'What you an' I went through that time makes us blood-brothers a dozen times over,' he remarked soberly. 'I'm throwin' in with you an' I won't hear any more protests!'

That night two old trail-partners slept in their blanket rolls beside the camp-fire.

The golden haze of morning in the south-west drifted on the wine-sweet air, and Will Callender was shaving his dark stubble, a chipped square of mirror propped against a rock. Old Lone-Star was crouching by the fire attending to the steaming coffee pot and a dixie of canned hash.

'Seems to me that if you're aimin' to buck this Tambaugh feller somethin' plumb decisive could be done about that blamed mine,' drawled the old-timer.

Callender canted his head at an inquisitive angle, trying to look at his old side-kick and steer the blade of his cutthroat around his chin at the same time.

'Meanin'?' he inquired.

'Meanin' I only worked in the mine for a couple of days, but I know my way around the camp an' I know that one of those cabins is near full of blastin' powder.'

'Well?'

'Well, if a few kegs of it was to find its way into the mouth of the shaft an' go sky-high, it'd be a plumb long time 'fore any ore was taken out of that stolen mine!'

'How many men are there at the mine site?'

' 'Bout a dozen.'

'Big odds.'

'Not too big for the two *hombres* who held off thirty lead-slingin' hellions back in the Dragoons!'

Will rinsed the lather from his chin in a dented can of water. 'You suggestin' we should ride into Silica Ridge an' blow up the mine in broad daylight?'

'In broad daylight, this very day, Will,' grinned the grizzled old Texan. 'It'd maybe make Cy Tambaugh realize you're no hot-headed young fool an' you're talkin' honest injun when you say you aim to buck him an' his rough-shod-ridin' outfit! '

'An' maybe bring him a couple of steps nearer comin' crawlin', spillin' the truth about Bob's killin'!' mused Will.

# FOUR

Allowing their horses to pick their way steadily along the shaly drifts of the semi-desert land, Will and Lone-Star rode easily in the direction of Silica Ridge. They sat their saddles in silence for long stretches at a time, but an occasional chuckle escaped the whisker-fringed lips of the peg-legged oldster every once in a while. Lone-Star had a spirit of Rebel devilry that stemmed from his honestly-held Texan opinion that one man from Texas way was worth at least two of any other locality on the continent. Riding towards an appointment with danger the old man's devil-may-care nature was in its element.

Will Callender rode with his hands fondling the butts of his low-slung Colts. He was riding to attempt a bold play against the men who worked the mine stolen from his murdered brother. He was riding into the very place where his easy-going, likeable kid brother died at the hands of vicious riders who outnumbered the kid by large odds and killed him, with the cloak of the law as a guise for their actions. Instinctively Callender knew the very atmosphere of the place would be a challenge to his fast-trigger nature; he felt his guns would bark at Silica Ridge before the plan he and his grizzled old companion of the lawdog trails had settled on was completed.

From his experience as a worker at the mine, old Lone-Star Dobbins had calculated that the best time to jump the miners would be at the moment the day's work was about to begin.

'Git them while there's still some sleep in their eyes, Will,' he had suggested, 'an' we'll make 'em think we're either a bad dream or a hallucination brought on by the cook's lousy breakfast.'

The golden orb of the sun was now well in the ascendancy, climbing against a cloudless, azure backdrop. The two riders topped a ridge from which they could see the mining camp, with two or three half-asleep figures moving about it, close at hand.

A few more minutes of riding and they were entering the mine site. A number of work-garbed figures were issuing from the two new-looking shacks, staring inquisitively at the two riders. One of them, a beefy man in gear more suited to the cattle range than a mining camp, came bow-legging over towards the grim-faced pair as they rode into the camp.

He was a flabby-faced man, bull-necked and with an ugly expanse of face weathered and sun-punished to the colour of mahogany.

'Waal,' he drawled, a grin that lacked humour splitting his features, 'if it ain't ole Peg-leg! What brings you back here, old-timer? Only yesterday you told me I could go to hell an' take the mine with me – who's your friend, incidentally?'

He stood there, thumbs hooked in cartridge-belt, head inquiringly on one side and rocking on the outside edges of his high-heeled boots. A Colt .44 was buckled close to his paunchy middle, too high for an effective draw in an emergency. Will Callender sized up this *hombre* as a blustering bully. He was no gunfighter, but he was the sort who would use his beef on a man – preferably if that man was smaller than he and held down by two more!

The remaining miners stood about in knots, watching the pair who had just ridden in. The stamp of the gunslinger that was worn so plainly by the bigger rider did not escape them. Certain of them too were uneasy about the resemblance this rangy gun-packer bore to another man who had died under their guns in the cabin that stood ominously lonesome on this mine site.

The big beefy man was dull-witted to the extent that he had not yet noted the mark of the gunfighter or the resemblance to Bob Callender. He stood there, holding his audacious pose as the mounted pair drew rein only a yard or so from him.

Lone-Star Dobbins sat his old horse with an amused smile struggling from the cover of his straggly whiskers. Will Callender sat with his lean hands crossed contentedly on the pommel of his saddle.

'Mister Chet Conners,' began the one-legged old Texan. 'I'll be frank an' to the point with you by tellin' you fust-off that we done come here to make trouble – that answers your question as to why we're here. In the second place, since you all must be plumb out of touch with what's goin' on around these parts, let me introduce you to a gent that made his presence felt in Crimson Peak yesterday – Mr Will Callender.' The oldster finished his introduction with a courtly flourish of a horny hand in the direction of Will.

Conners stopped rocking on the edges of his feet. Over his face spread an expression similar to that reflected on the features of Jake Kurdia when Will had announced his identity in the café the previous day.

'Callender!' he half whispered. Then he made a hamfisted grab for the gun at his paunch.

Will Callender straightened in the saddle. His hands went through the rapid-draw motions that had been witnessed by Tambaugh and his cronies in the Palacio Hotel the day before. Chet Conners had not even started his draw and the mouths of Callender's Colts were levelled squarely at his head. He dropped his clumsy hand away from the butt of the weapon.

There was a restless shuffle among a knot of miners standing to one side. Lone-Star drew his own guns and covered the group.

'You-all better congregate yourselves into one parcel,' ordered the old-timer, with a motion of a Colt. 'Git yourselves into one herd so I can keep my eye on you!'

Sullenly the miners, all of whom were unarmed, clustered into a single group.

'W-what do you want here?' faltered Chet Conners. As Will had figured, he was a man who would show yellow and he now looked completely scared.

There was a sardonic smile on Callender's lean face when he swung down from the saddle of his palomino, still covering Chet Conners.

'Like Lone-Star told you, Conners, we came to make trouble,' he answered. 'You an' your boys keep yourselves to yourselves and you won't come to much harm but your boss, Tambaugh, is goin' to find it kinda hard to get at his silver lode when we're through!'

'You better clear out,' blustered the mine-camp foreman, 'or you'll likely find yourself in the same place as your brother when Mister Tambaugh catches up with you!'

Something approaching a snarl twisted Will Callender's lean features at this. Even Lone-Star, who had seen the tall Arizonan with bucking six-guns in the midst of bullet-bitten Arizona Ranger actions, had never witnessed such savagery written on Will's face at the mention of his dead brother.

He advanced on Chet Conners with slow steps, stopping inches from him and prodding his ample paunch with a Colt barrel.

'What do you know about the death of my brother, Conners?' Tiny flames seemed to glimmer in the grey eyes of the man from Arizona as he asked the question. There was a mounting tension among the watching Tambaugh miners, lined up under the Lone-Star Dobbins' guns.

Will prodded the beefy man's paunch again.

'Talk, damn you! Were you in on the killin' of my brother?'

Chet Conners' fleshy face was studded with drops of perspiration.

'He was shot by a marshal's posse – resistin' arrest,' he mouthed.

'Change your tune!' rasped Will. 'I didn't ask for the alibi you Tambaugh snakes keep spittin' out – I asked you if you were there. Were you? Tell me, or I'll put a slug into your yellow hide!'

'Yes,' croaked the flabby mine foreman. 'I was in the posse under Marshal Collis. It was legal, Callender. Bob Callender robbed the Crimson Peak Bank and killed the teller. We tailed him out here an' he resisted us with a carbine. He was shot resistin' the law – it was legal—' Conners' words were spluttered, one tripping over the other, until Will cut him short with another forceful prod of both guns.

'You're talkin' too fast an' makin' no impression,' he told Conners. 'How many of these other *hombres*, if any, rode with that posse? If there's any in that bunch who had a hand in what happened here three months ago, point them out – pronto!'

Chet Conners was quaking visibly as he raised a hand and pointed to a scowling man among those old Lone-Star was holding in check from his sway-backed horse.

'He was there,' denounced the yellow mine foreman.

'Name him!' ordered Will flatly. 'Name him if you don't want a bellyful of lead!'

'Ed Costain.'

Will took in the features of the man, filing them away in his mind, a knack learned over his years of service with the Arizona Rangers.

'I'll remember you, Costain,' he murmured, then to Conners: 'Who else was there, lardbelly?'

Chet Conners pointed out a slim, lantern-jawed youngster, a kid of hardly more than twenty.

'Him too – Milt Walker.'

'I'll remember your face, kid,' said Will, taking stock of the youth as he had of Costain. 'Who else, Conners?'

Chet Conners was almost blubbering under the threat of the guns held against his middle; he pointed out two more men in miner's garb. They looked hard cases, unsavoury border riff-raff. If looks had lethal power, the glances this pair and Ed Costain were bestowing on Conners as he named them would have made a corpse of the flabby mine foreman on the spot.

'Those two,' Conners told the tall Arizonan. 'Wally Gifford an' Dave la Platte. They were there, an' that's all.'

There were twin bayonet points in Will Callender's eyes. 'I heard there was more like a dozen men in that posse – all Tambaugh's men.'

'There were others, but they're not here, they're back at the CT ranch.'

'Names!' demanded Will.

'Lou Killan, Slim Wheaton, Ace Pocock, Mex Chavez, an' Rudy Steptoe,' named Conners.

'That all?'

'That's all, I swear it,' blubbed Conners.

'I'll remember the names,' promised Callender. 'An' who was the *hombre* who wore clothin' similar to my brother's? The guy who rode Bob's horse – I mean the *hombre* who was paid by Cy Tambaugh to hold up the Crimson Peak Bank – the bank Tambaugh owns himself – an' shoot the teller who was himself paid by Tambaugh. You just uncinch your fat tongue some more, Conners, an' tell me that!'

Conners swallowed hard and clenched his teeth, but another impatient prod from Will Callender brought answer from him.

'It was Clay Galliver,' he spluttered.

'Who's he?'

'Deputy marshal at Crimson Peak!'

'So,' growled Will. 'I should have killed him yesterday.' Inwardly he reflected that the youth who packed a deputy's star was of similar build to his dead brother and would easily pass for him if he was wearing his clothes and heavily masked.

Will bestowed a kick on the side of Conners' leg and motioned towards the group of miners Lone-Star was watching with a quick jerk of his head.

'Get over there, lardbelly. Stand with your friends an' keep quiet.' To Lone-Star Dobbins, he called: 'Where's the blastin' powder stored?'

'The older shack up that way a piece,' replied the oldster without removing his eyes from the Tambaugh men under his vigilance.

It was something of a shock to Will to realize that this was the original shack at Silica Ridge, the one his brother had built and the one in which he had met his death. Holstering his guns, Callender walked towards the building. It was solidly built and seemed to reflect something of the practical, hard-working nature of Bob Callender. Will walked around the outside of the wooden structure, examining the weathered timberings. There were no bullet scars in evidence, which was unusual for a place in which a posse was supposed to have laid siege to a desperate criminal.

Kicking open the door, Will entered. The interior of the shack was piled with boxes and oddments of mining equipment. Over in one corner stood several kegs of explosive and some lengths of fuse. It was in crossing towards these that the Arizonan caught sight of the disused bunk affixed to the wall.

Will stopped in his tracks and caught his breath with a gasp, for the bunk, now stripped of its bedding, held the truth of Bob Callender's killing. On its timbers and on the wall to which it was affixed, still new-looking, were a dozen or so bullet scars. There were even holes where slugs had lodged in the wood, but someone who must have had half a conscience had pulled the lead out.

So they had come upon Bob in the night and killed him as he lay in his blankets! Prior to seeing the evidence of the bullet-punished bunk, Will, for some reason which he himself would have been unable to explain, was prepared to think the Tambaugh riders had given Bob something of a fighting chance before gunning him down. But it had not been so – it had been absolute butchery!

Will Callender had spent several days riding around the vicinity of Crimson Peak before showing up in the town, investigating in quiet but thorough Arizona Ranger fashion. Out of a score of conversations in saloons and beside round-up chuck wagons and camp-fires in towns and on ranges that were near enough to Tambaugh's country to hear of the doings there and yet were not under Tambaugh's sway, he had pieced together the story of the alleged bank robbery. The main story-line was that a figure, identified by its build and clothing as that of Bob Callender, came thundering into Crimson Peak on Bob's familiar mount during the late afternoon. The hold-up had been swift and had occurred while Crimson Peak was deep in its drowsy afternoon indolence.

Almost before the revolver shots that had killed teller Henry Dirks had shaken the desert-edge township from its siesta, the man who looked like Bob was seen riding out the way he had entered at a hurtling pace. Marshal Roy Collis, better known to Will as back-shooting Lafe Askew, had found little difficulty in organising a posse of Tambaugh's CT wranglers who just happened to be in town. Bob had been trailed by the riders to his camp on Silica Ridge and had been finally killed by the posse after resisting fiercely from his shack.

That was the story. Now Will read the truth in the bullet scars and pocks around the bunk. The ruse had been planned cleverly and timed with deadly effect. It would be early evening by the time the Tambaugh riders had reached Silica Ridge after Clay Galliver, in the guise of Bob Callender, had killed Henry Dirks and gone through the motions of robbing the bank.

Those riders, who came here intent on butchery to effect Tambaugh's grabbing of Bob's silver lode, would arrive to find the young prospector sleeping in his bunk after a hard day's work. So easy to pump bullets into a sleeping man! So easy to return to Crimson Peak and tell the townsfolk that the man who had stolen their money and killed one of their number had finally been slain after putting up desperate resistance.

Lips drawn in a tight line, Will Callender picked up three kegs of blasting powder and a length of fuse. He carried the kegs outside, where his old partner of the Arizona law-trails was still keeping the glowering Tambaugh men under check with his Colts. He walked down the slight incline from the cabin to the main area of the camp where the group of men stood.

The black opening to the mine workings stood to their back, and a rough corral of peeled posts standing a little to one side, held a dozen horses. Will walked deliberately towards this, opened wide the swinging section that served as a gate and hazed the animals out with a series of cowboy whoops. They scattered, clattering away among the rocks. Will pulled a six-gun and fired a couple of shots to throw a scare that would speed them on their way into them.

He high-heeled his way towards the shaft mouth, carrying the small kegs under an arm. It was satisfying to know that these Tambaugh men would be stranded out in this neck of the woods for some time until they caught their stampeded horses.

'If anyone's down this mine,' he called towards the men under the old Texan's guns, 'you'd better tell me pronto or they're gonna he entombed!'

'Ain't nobody down there,' came the voice of Chet Conners, grating and surly.

Drawing his bowie knife, Will widened a split between the slats on the tops of each keg. He snicked off three short lengths of fuse, tamped them into the apertures he had made and carried the kegs some three yards into the mouth of the mine. He stacked them side by side on the dirt floor, hard against the propped-up wall.

He struck a match and touched the flame in quick succession to each frayed end of fuse, then he was legging it, spurs a-jingling, out of the mouth of the mine workings.

'Short fuses!' he bellowed. 'Better scatter!'

No sooner were the words out of his mouth than he was forking his palomino. He and his peg-legged old companion wheeled their mounts swiftly, speeding them with loud verbal urgings.

.

Leaving the Tambaugh men to scatter for the cover of the rocks, Will and Lone-Star thundered out of the mine camp at Silica Ridge. Behind them, before they were lost among the sun-split rock formations, a six-gun slammed out three shots and the riders heard the spat of slugs whanging off the rocks.

That would be Conners, the only one of the miners who was armed, trying to put up some sort of show for the benefit of the men who had seen his yellow streak under Callender's gun.

About half a minute of hard riding and the shattering boom of the explosion came blasting from behind Will and Lone-Star. They turned in their saddles and saw a great spout of earth gushing up against the azure sky in a ragged splash.

The pair urged their mounts forward until they topped a rise, paused and looked back, twisting their bodies about in their saddles. From this point they could see Silica Ridge. The mouth of the mine-shaft had disappeared into a pile of debris, over which a heavy pall of dust drifted. The figures of Chet Conners and his men were to be seen running aimlessly about.

Lone-Star Dobbins gave another of his Texas Rebel yells.

'Kicked 'em,' he enthused in his corncrake voice. 'We rode into their back-yard an' kicked their shirt-tails! Man, how I wish I had a bottle of Crow so we could celebrate!'

# FIVE

That night Will and Lone-Star made camp at a different location in the gaunt uplands above Crimson Peak. There was no spring to provide water here, but both men had filled their big desert-riders' canteens before leaving the previous camp site. They were now living on the remaining supplies Lone-Star still had in his big prospector's war-sack.

They spent the greater part of the day sheltering from the white blaze of the sun under the gnarled rock formations. Old Lone-Star constantly rejoiced over the snook they had cocked at the Tambaugh faction by blowing up the entrance to the mine.

'So darned easy,' he enthused. 'Just a matter of riding in on them an' the whole darned scheme worked smooth as a well-oiled Winchester! By cracky – how I wish I had a bottle of whiskey to drink to us an' the downfall of Cy Tambaugh!'

Will Callender, lying under a craggy rock, Stetson tipped over his face, took a less jubilant view of the wrecking of the Silica Ridge mine. It had been a success, sure, but it had been a mere episode in his personal war ou Tambaugh.

The significance of the bullet-scarred bunk in the cabin that had been the home of his brother niggled at his susceptibilities like an old wound, gnawing persistently. Equally rankling too was the knowledge that he had been in the presence of men who had been in the posse that day three months ago and had left them still alive.

But there was little he could do then and there, he reflected. The men at the mine had been unarmed and he was not the one to shoot down enemies without giving them a fighting chance.

Their time would come later. Meanwhile, the names of those who had a hand in the butchering of his kid brother were impressed on his lawman's memory: Ed Costain, Milt Walker, Wally Gifford and Dave la Platte. They had been at the mine, he knew their names and their faces. Then there were the others, at the CT spread: Lou Killan, Slim Wheaton, Ace Pocock, Mex Chavez and Rudy Steptoe, mere names as yet – but he would meet up with them one day!

Stretching in the shade, reaching for the makings of a rice-paper Bull Durham smoke, Will reflected that grasping Cy Tambaugh had been deprived, however temporarily, of his ill-gotten silver ore; and that was something to notch up on the progress sheet of his campaign against Tambaugh.

Lone-Star Dobbins found that one corner of the

adobe and wooden cluster that was Crimson Peak could be seen from their camp site. The town had a fascination for him, the kind of fascination that lights and life and saloons held for a man who had been long weeks on the desert, seeking the ever-elusive lucky strike.

Throughout the long, searing afternoon, the oldster stared at the unlovely straggle of squat build-ings, diminutive in the blued distance of the desert edge.

'A bottle of Old Crow would be plumb enchant-ing right now,' the old man kept opining. 'I figure a trip down to that little ole burg would be in order right now.'

'But not wise until the ruckus we caused by blowin' the daylights outta that mine has blown over some, you whiskey guzzlin' old goat!' Will told him.

The one-legged old Texan continued to gaze at the distant town wistfully. Whisky was nectar to him, and his long lay-off from alcohol while on the desert had given him a nagging craving under the belt-buckle.

The afternoon grew chill, long purple shadows slanted through the gnarled rocks and night began to drift over the craggy land as the blood-red orb of the sun went down over the desert rim.

Will and Lone-Star rolled into their blankets beside a fire newly fed with greasewood. With the ability to sleep anywhere at the drop of a hat, acquired over years of range riding and following the Ranger-trails, Will was soon snoring lightly.

Lone-Star Dobbins shifted restlessly. The craving for a drink was grinding under his belt with a stronger intensity. He licked his cracked, whisker-fringed lips with a dry tongue and looked up at the myriad stars in the blue-black bowl of the desert sky.

They looked cool and liquid and set Lone-Star to thinking of drink again.

'By cracky!' the old-timer grunted, half aloud, 'why shouldn't I ride to Crimson Peak for a drink?'

He put the proposition to himself and built up an argument on it.

Why shouldn't he go in search of the Old Crow he was craving? That was the errand he had been on when he happened upon Will the day before, anyway. So what if he would be sticking his nose into Tambaugh's town?

He'd shucked around for sixty and some odd years, hadn't he? He'd always been able to take care of himself and wasn't dead yet, though he'd come damn' close to it often enough. He'd survived the Texas cattle drives, four years as a Confederate Army cavalry trooper, more years than he could remember of cow wrangling, and a long, hazardous spell as an Arizona Ranger.

By cracky, he'd lived through all that and he'd live through more. He'd ride into Tambaugh's town, have himself a few drinks and come out with a whole skin – but it might be better if he didn't waken Will and let him know he was going.

Will would probably disapprove – anyway, why disturb the young fellow's sleep?

He'd ride quietly out, have his drinks and ride quietly back to camp again. He rose silently, buckled on his pegleg, pulled on his single boot and crammed his old, floppy sombrero on his head.

Lone-Star had a slight qualm of conscience as he led his old sway-backed horse out of the camp. He looked back over his shoulder and saw that his partner was still sleeping soundly.

The oldster dismissed the qualm of conscience and led his horse out of camp.

After some twenty minutes of riding he struck a trail that snaked away in the direction of Crimson Peak. The moon was high now, silvering the gaunt land. Lone-Star Dobbins rode steadily, purposefully and licking his lips in happy anticipation.

Shortly before reaching the desert-edge town, he paused at a point where the trail split an isolated grove of stunted live oaks, his attention caught by something white on the bole of one of the trees. It was a poster, placed so that it would be easily discernible to anyone who passed along the trail.

Riding up to the tree, the old cripple stopped and screwed his eyes to scan the rough hand lettering, easily readable in the moonlight:

'Wanted – alive! Will Callender, brother of the notorious Bob Callender, for the shooting of Deputy Galliver, of Crimson Peak. This man is armed and highly dangerous, but is wanted alive by the local law authority. A substantial reward will be paid for his apprehension. Roy Collis, Town Marshal, Crimson Peak.'

The wizened old Texan grinned at the signature. The signature might be that of the back-shooting Arizona renegade, Lafe Askew, who now used a different name, but it was clear that the so-called 'local law authority' was simply Cy Tambaugh.

Tambaugh wanted the big Arizonan alive because he had admitted having certain mysterious information in which the local cattle baron and grafter was interested.

The poster was a longshot, posted in the hope that someone would be foolish enough to go bounty-hunting after Callender.

Lone-Star spat energetically. Will would have himself a loud belly-laugh when he saw the poster, he mused. Then he spurred his old mount onwards to Crimson Peak – and whiskey.

There had been a time when Jake Kurdia had been a rider for Tambaugh's CT outfit. That was before his leg had been crippled by the slashing horns of a maddened longhorn steer. Now he ran a crummy eating-house in Crimson Peak.

Kurdia was still a Tambaugh man and his restaurant was often used as something of a town branch for Tambaugh's activities. Tambaugh riders usually gathered there when in town.

Since Cy Tambaugh had taken over the silver workings of the ill-fated Bob Callender the restaurant had become doubly important as the miners' nearest point of contact with Tambaugh. It became a sort of half-way house, since the CT ranch-house lay a number of miles on the opposite side of town to where the mine workings were situated. Messages left at the café by men from the mine would eventually be collected and taken to Tambaugh by CT riders stopping off on their trips into Crimson Peak. Cy Tambaugh relied largely on this arrangement to keep in touch with developments at the remote mine.

As evening sifted down over the town and Stella Rivers was tidying the café, five horses came thundering into town in a flurry of dust. Their riders hitched them at the rack outside the café and trooped in.

Stella caught her breath when she realized that they were Tambaugh men from the mine, led by flabby Chet Conners.

Conners' brow was black as he legged into the lamp-lit café, followed by Wally Gifford, Dave la Platte, Milt Walker and Ed Costain.

'Fix us some coffee!' ordered Conners harshly. 'Where's Kurdia?'

At that moment Jake Kurdia, attracted by the concentrated pounding of boot heels, opened the door of the establishment's living quarters and limped into the café.

'What's wrong?' he wanted to know. The fact that all the miners were wearing guns and had the obvious look of being out of sorts to no mean extent puzzled the café owner.

'That Callender feller has been to the mine an' blown the shaft to hell an' gone!' Chet Conners snorted. 'Him an' an ole peg-legged coot from Texas

that worked at the mine for a coupla days rode in
this mornin' an' pulled a fast one on us with no trouble at all!'

Stella Rivers, dishing out coffee for the miners,
felt a thrill at this information. The tall man from
Arizona who had come to this territory to openly set
himself against the might of Cy Tambaugh had been
much on her mind since the previous day.

It was gratifying to hear that he had got this far in
his war on Tambaugh. That buck-toothed little blus-
terer, Clay Galliver, was walking around town with a
shattered arm because of him and now he had
blown up the mine that had been stolen from his
young brother.

There had been a time when the girl with the
raven hair had been fully sure that the man who had
ridden out of town after shooting the teller at the
bank was Bob Callender. Now she was certain that
the tall, courtly man who had come into town the
previous day was right and the whole episode had
been a cunning move by Tambaugh to seize the
young prospector's silver strike. Wholeheartedly she
was on the side of Will Callender in his battle against
the law-unto-itself element that had held the whip-
hand in this corner of New Mexico for far too long.

'Where you headed now?' asked Jake Kurdia.

'Out to the CT to tell Mister Tambaugh.'

'It happened this mornin' an' you're only just
goin' to Tambaugh?'

'Yeah. They ran off our cayuses an' we had a
helluva chase catchin' them. Then we attempted to

shift the rubble an' open the mine some, but it'll take days of work,' glowered Conners.

'Looks like you was made to look a pack of fools,' observed Kurdia.

Chet Conners winced. He had been forced to show his yellow streak that morning and had not forgotten it. Nor had the men under him.

'I figure we'll make Callender an' his side-kick into two fools when we go after 'em,' rejoined the mine foreman. 'Mr Tambaugh will send a bunch of the boys from the CT to help us get 'em. We'll make 'em into two fools all right – two plumb dead fools!'

'Mister Tambaugh don't want Callender killed,' rejoined Jake Kurdia flatly.

'Don't want him killed – why not?' It was Ed Costain who asked the question.

'I don't know, but it seems Callender has somethin' on Mister Tambaugh. He strutted into the Palacio yesterday an' talked plumb big. He told Collis he was a back-shootin' owlhooter from Arizona an' Collis was almighty scared of him. Then Clay Galliver tried to draw on him an' Callender shot him up – he drew like greased lightnin'.'

'We've seen him draw,' growled Dave la Platte. 'He drew on us this mornin' – he's fast, all right!'

'Why don't Mister Tambaugh want him killed?' persisted Chet Conners.

'I don't know,' replied the leathery-faced café proprietor. 'Callender seemed to be holdin' somethin' over him. He mentioned some woman's name an' it made Mister Tambaugh go all soft – never seen him like that before! Some woman named Rosalind.'

'So Mister Tambaugh don't want this Callender killed.' grumbled Wally Gifford. 'What are we supposed to do – let him go around shootin' us up like he shot young Galliver up an' blowin' things sky-high like he did that mine? What's wrong with Tambaugh? He usta make a big show of runnin' this territory with an iron hand, now he's prepared to let this Callender hellion run foot-loose an' gunhappy all around the place!'

'I don't know what's gotten into Mister Tambaugh. All I know is Callender is holdin' some-thin' over him, it must be somethin' from years back, an' Mister Tambaugh wants him bringin' in alive,' replied Jake Kurdia testily.

Dave la Platte, standing by the counter and only a matter of inches from the grimy window, clattered his empty coffee cup down on the counter roughly.

'Gimme another dose of that java, girlie!' he ordered.

Stella Rivers, used to the discourtesy of these Tambaugh riders, took the cup and began to refill it in silence. She pushed it across the counter with a delicate but workstained hand.

Dave la Platte ignored the replenished coffee cup. He was standing with his hands on his hips, staring out of the window with a broken-toothed grin split-ting his unlovely countenance.

'Why, lookit here!' he almost yelled. 'Mister Tambaugh may want Callender alive, but here's one bird we can pluck *muy pronto*!'

The gun-hung Tambaugh miners hastened to the window. Ed Costain gave a low, triumphant whistle at what he saw, while the sight drew an animal-like grunt from Chet Conners. Stella stole a glance into the moon-washed street through the only portion of the window not obscured by big-hatted heads.

She saw the moonbeam-whitened spread of the dusty street and the Palacio Hotel immediately opposite the café. Yellow lamplight bloomed from the windows of the hotel, splashing across the wooden gallery and illuminating the old man who was this minute dismounting stiffly from a sway-back old horse at the hitch-rail outside the hotel.

He was a stranger to Stella Rivers, a stooped old man with the look of the prospector about him. She could see that his right leg had been replaced by a stout wooden peg. The girl remembered what Chet Conners had told her uncle about Will Callender blowing up the mine at Silica Ridge with the aid of a peg-legged old man from Texas, and a cold rush of terror welled up inside her, possessing every atom of her being.

The gun-carrying miners from Silica Ridge converged on the door without a word, but the girl could see their intent written on their hard, stubbled faces. They were out to shoot down the old cripple out on the street!

She hastened around the counter, the skirt of her shabby dress swirling. Dave la Platte already had the door open and was stepping out on to the boardwalk, grabbing for his gun, Chet Conners was close behind him. The old man across the street was stumping up the couple of scuffed steps giving on to the gallery of the Palacio, his stooped back presented to his would-be killers.

Stella thrust her slight form between Chet Conners and Wally Gifford, who was following the mine foreman out of the door; she grabbed the edge of the open door, trying to make a barrier with her arm.

'No!' she breathed brokenly. 'You can't do it!'

Wally Gifford thrust her arm down with a pair of horny paws.

Someone grabbed her about the shoulders, pulling her back so the portal was no longer obstructed. She had a brief and hazy glimpse of the old man, now on the gallery of the hotel.

Stella screamed on a high note: 'Look out, old man! Look—!'

Jake Kurdia, who had grabbed his niece about the shoulders, clamped a hand over her mouth, stifling her shrill warning. He dragged her into the interior of the café and the remaining miners spilled on to the boardwalk with naked guns.

# SIX

From the bowels of the Palacio Hotel a badly-tuned piano tinkled out the strains of 'Marchin' Through Georgia'.

It was a damn' Yankee tune, reflected Lone-Star Dobbins, but he could put the war behind him and let bygones be bygones as well as the next fellow. Besides, this was the first drinking establishment in Crimson Peak. Friendly light rayed from over the batwing doors and two signs reading 'Beers' and 'Whisky' were discernible in the mixture of lamp-light and moonglow.

The first left Lone-Star unmoved, but the second was an invitation he could not resist.

He swung his substitute limb over the back of his ancient mount, threw the reins in a hitch over the rack fronting the gallery of the Palacio.

The oldster stumped up the steps and on to the wooden gallery.

From behind him came a sudden sound. A door

opening quickly, squeaking as the sun-warped doors
of this land always squeaked because of the gritty
sand that got into the hinges, the clatter of boots
and the climax of a woman's voice shrilling:

'Look out, old man! Look—!'

Lone-Star whirled, streaking for the Colts at his
belt with a swiftness that had been learned in the
free-wheeling days of the Texas cattle drives and had
not been impaired by the weight of his years. He saw
two men, shadowy and gun-flourishing, on the
boardwalk across the rutted, moon-splashed vista of
the street. Others were spilling out of the lamp-
yellowed oblong of the café door.

A gun spouted red flame and a bullet whanged
into a stanchion of the hotel gallery, shattering slivers of dry wood.

Lone-Star retreated to the rear of the gallery, triggering both guns and cursing the encumbrance of
his wooden leg.

He heard a yelp from the opposite boardwalk and
a hoarse voice that he recognized as Chet Conners'
howled something about being hit. The oldster saw
a heavy figure lurch against an upright supporting
the awning over the opposite boardwalk. He fired
again, and no sooner had Chet Conners pitched life-
lessly into the street than the flat clatter of gunfire
from three or four guns echoed out.

Lone-Star threw himself down in the face of the
blazing slashes of flame. The withering hail of lead
starred the light-backed window of the Palacio, but
the old Texan felt the burning thrust of a slug

driving into his left shoulder.

He had to get into a darker spot on this gallery – too much damned light!

Down on the floor of the gallery the old-timer fired three times through the interstices of the rail at the group of shadowy figures fanning out on the boardwalk opposite. The slug in his shoulder was aching furiously, but he forced a jubilant laugh from his lips as he saw two of the figures buckle to the boardwalk.

Answering fire bellowed from the Tambaugh men, but they could no longer see the old man now he was on the floor of the gallery, and the whining lead spatted into the facade of the Palacio. Lone-Star Dobbins rolled over on to his back and propelled himself along the scuffed boards with his sound leg.

He was at the open end of the gallery now and lying flat on his back.

He lay there thumbing cartridges from the loops at his belt into the empty chambers of his guns. There was a long instant of silence in which the shadowy figures across the street moved urgently about the boardwalk.

One of the two men he had just hit struggled weakly to his feet and made for the deep shadows close to the café wall; the other man remained a crumpled, lifeless form.

Lone-Star lay watching, allowing the injured man to gain the obscurity of the shadows without firing on him.

'I think we got him!' yelled a thin voice. 'He's gone awful quiet.' Lone-Star lay on the hotel gallery setting his broken stumps of teeth against the increasing nag of the wound in his shoulder.

He waited, knowing he could not be seen from across the street, lying as he was on the boards of this shadowy end of the hotel gallery, where it gave on to a trash-littered alley.

'Yeah,' the voice came again. 'I figure we got the ole hellion.'

Two big-hatted silhouettes came off the board-walk by the café and began to cross towards the Palacio. Lone-Star Dobbins levelled his guns from his awkward angle of fire and split the night air with two ragged red shards of muzzle-flame. Through the acrid, eye-stinging drift of cordite he saw one of the figures spin about in his tracks and fall flat on his face; the other went scooting for the shadows from which he had emerged as fast as his legs would take him. Instantly a fusillade of whining lead came spitting at the old cripple's position. He fired back aimlessly and knowing he must shift his position pronto now that the Tambaugh gunmen had his whereabouts marked.

The old-timer rolled over on to his belly, lying hard against the wooden wall of the hotel. Using his hands and his good leg to crawl off the gallery, he pulled himself into a crouch at the edge of the alley-way.

Hot lead was splatting around this end of the gallery now. A stray slug slapped into the old man's body just above the heart, sending the breath out of him in a whistling gasp.

He crouched open-mouthed in the dust, while a wave of crimson washed up before his eyes and a claw of agony tore at him.

He knew now there was no surviving the odds against him.

Lone~Star could make out the dim activity on the opposite side of the moon-whitened street. The hitched horses kicking nervously in the clamour of gunfire, the gun flourishing figures of his enemies over on the far boardwalk.

By grab! He wasn't going down without showing the kind of fight that was in a Texas man!

He gathered himself up, pulled his stooped body up to its full height and stumped boldly out of the alley entrance, guns flaming determinedly at the Tambaugh men.

He hoped Will would not think him too much of a fool for coming into the town this way – he would try to take as many of the Tambaugh bunch as possible with him for the sake of Will and his murdered kid brother.

Bullets from the opposing guns slashed at him mercilessly.

He sure was grateful to the woman who yelled the warning to him, whoever she was. He'd been a damned fool and he hadn't had that whiskey, either. He sure hoped Will would not blame him too much.

He was hobbling forward now, making a crazy, zigzagging one-man advance on the gunmen over by the eating-house, guns spitting fire and lead the whole time.

Maybe it was the best way to go after the kind of life he'd led, he told himself as he staggered into the crackle of opposing gunfire. Maybe it was a good thing he was going. He was getting old and a burden to himself. Every day he felt his bones growing a little weaker; every day it was more of an effort to drag his wooden limb around.

Lone-Star's six-guns were still barking when he pitched stiffly into the dust, face first.

Will Callender pulled rein to read the poster that adorned the stunted live-oak. The high moon laved the harsh land with its cold whiteness and painted deep shadows on the craggy face of the tall rider as it creased into a humour-lacking grin at the legend of the white square of paper.

So Tambaugh was trying to make an outlaw of him – an outlaw who was wanted alive for the shooting up of a peace officer. Will knew that the notice, although signed by the man who now chose to call himself Roy Collis, had been conceived by Cy Tambaugh. Tambaugh wanted him alive because of Rosalind, and it gave the big Arizonan a feeling of grim elation to know that Tambaugh would be ordering his men to attempt to take alive a swift gunhand such as he.

Tambaugh wanted him alive, at least until he had divulged what he knew of Rosalind.

Maybe it was wrong to bring Rosalind into this in

the way he was, and maybe he was a heel for doing so. But this was war against the schemer who had caused his younger brother to be murdered – bullet-pounded to death, as he now knew, while sleeping in his cabin.

By sheer coincidence he had something to hold over the head of Tambaugh, something from another time and place. In a war in which the odds were stacked against him to the highest extent, he felt justified in using the name of Rosalind.

The quirk of humour that the Wanted poster brought to Will's face had scarcely died away when the angry, distance-thinned crackle of gunfire came from the direction of the town, bringing Will's thoughts leaping back to the business he had in hand.

'Lone-Star!' he gasped, touching spurs to his palomino. 'I knew the old-timer would stick his nose into trouble.'

Urging the horse with spur jabs and handslaps, he went thundering towards Crimson Peak at a hurtling pace, raising a long wake of hoof-stirred dust.

Will had awakened only a short time after his old companion had left camp, realized that the oldster's sleeping gear was empty and put two and two together. Lone-Star had been harping about whiskey the whole of the day, and Will cursed himself for not realising that the old Texan, in one of his whiskey-craving moods, would go in search of liquor at whatever cost. Accordingly, Will had risen, saddled his mount and set off on the trail that could only lead to Crimson Peak. He knew too well that, after the episode at Silica Ridge, there would be danger for the old timer if he ventured to Cy Tambaugh's town.

Now it seemed Lone-Star was in the midst of trouble – and serious trouble, if the angry, sustained blaze of distant shooting was any guide.

Callender rode like fury, splitting the night wind and urging every ounce of energy out of the palomino. Up ahead the sounds of gunfire ebbed and flowed, spurring the Arizonan to beat the horse onward. He rimmed the crest of a ridge on the snorting palomino, swept down a drift along which the trail ribboned towards the huddle of buildings that was Crimson Peak.

Above the thunder of his animal's hooves, he could still hear the sounds of firing, coming in a long, continuous distance-flattened clatter, as though many guns were barking at once.

Now Will was nearing the town, and the gunfire ceased abruptly. There was a terrible finality about this stopping of the angry sounds of battle that caused the man from Arizona to touch his spurs deep into the flanks of his horse.

There was an ominous silence hanging on the air as Callender thundered into town. Passing Rittendon's livery barn he could see clusters of people standing around still forms lying in the dust. The pale rays of the moon illumined the scene with a cold whiteness, giving a high effect of death and tragedy. Silent figures were issuing from buildings to group inquisitively about the still forms, now that the shooting was over.

Will slowed his horse to a walk. His right hand wavered close to a Colt as he rode into the town, taking in the scene of recent, violent activity.

He passed Kurdia's café. The boardwalk outside the eating-house was deserted, but the still form of burly Chet Conners was sprawled half on and half off the plank-walk. Another corpse lay by the café doorway with a bunch of townsfolk standing about it. The inquisitive folk drifted away hastily at the approach of the tall gun-hung man on the walking palomino. Passing the eating-house, Callender bestowed a bleak glance on the dead man.

Then he moved his mount in the direction of the group of Crimson Peak citizenry grouped about another shapeless bundle lying in the centre of the rutted street a few yards from the Palacio Hotel. They dispersed at his approach. The reputation of the tall gunhand who had openly bucked Cy Tambaugh and shattered Clay Galliver's arm had spread through the little town; the more peace-loving people of the desert-edge settlement were apprehensive of such a man arriving, gun-hung, on the very heels of a bullet banquet.

Callender, without dismounting, gazed down at the crumpled figure in the dust. The floppy old sombrero was still on his head and both arms were stretched forward in death, still holding the pair of Colts, pointing them in the direction of Kurdia's beanery as though in accusation.

Poor Lone-Star! He was too good a man to come to this kind of end, but he surely gave the Tambaugh hawks bullet trouble before he cashed in, mused Will.

With his mouth set in a tight line he wheeled the palomino and danced it across the street in the direction of Kurdia's restaurant. The inquisitive Crimson Peak folk, sensing that this night's gunplay had not yet concluded, began to make themselves scarce. Callender threw his reins over the rack outside the eating-establishment and dismounted. He drew both Colts and stepped on to the board-walk, making not for the door of the café, but for the square of grimy window backed by the yellow bloom of lamplight. Edging close to the heat-warped clap-board wall, he stole a glance into the café.

He saw Wally Gifford sprawled over the counter holding his jaw. Blood seeped through his fingers in crimson threads. Dave la Platte was squatting in a rickety chair clutching a shoulder, his features held in a frozen wince.

Milt Walker was squatting beside him. The lantern-jawed youngster was dressing a bullet wound on La Platte's ankle.

Lafe Askew, in his parsonical marshal's get-up, was standing by the counter with his buck-toothed young deputy, Clay Galliver, his right arm in a sling, nearby.

Stella Rivers stood close to the door leading to the living quarters of the café, and an enraged Jake Kurdia was shaking her roughly, gripping her shoul-der with a grubby paw.

'. . . you little fool! Why did you have to shout out that way? The old-timer was nothin' to you. You put him on his guard an' look how he shot the boys up!' Callender heard him rasp.

It took Will only a second to take in the scene and hear the words of the girl's uncle through the grimy, cracked glass. Then he ducked swiftly away from the window and kicked open the door of the eating-house.

He stood on the threshold, Colts levelled into the lamplit café and a dangerous smoulder in his grey eyes.

'Reach for the rafters – all of you!' he grated.

# SEVEN

Under the threat of Callender's guns Jake Kurdia loosened his grip on Stella and took a hasty step backwards. He stood against the wall baring his teeth in a grin of fear. The faces of each of the Tambaugh gunmen froze into masks of surprise and each held his pose rigidly.

Callender surveyed the scene of wounded humanity, noting with inward satisfaction that only the town marshal of Crimson Peak and the youngster, Milt Walker, appeared to be uninjured. Old Lone-Star had handed out plenty of fight before they gunned him down.

Marshal Roy Collis, alias Lafe Askew, flattened himself against the wall next to the café proprietor. His wounded kid deputy stood beside him, a twist of hate holding his Billy the Kid features.

'Listen, Callender,' began Askew, breathlessly, 'me an' Galliver weren't in on this, we just came—'

'Put a hobble on your tongue!' ordered Will

Callender. 'I'll do the talking from here on in. Get against that wall, the whole bunch of you. Miss Rivers, stand behind the counter out of harm's way.'

Obeying Callender's order, emphasized with a wave of a business-like Colt, the Tambaugh miners ranged themselves against the wall. Callender noted that Jake Kurdia was not wearing a gun.

'Were you in on this gunfest, Kurdia?' he asked.

'No – I swear I wasn't, Callender! I never pulled a trigger on the old-timer!'

Callender motioned for him to stand to one side. Lafe Askew, possessed with the fear that this bleak-eyed Arizonan was about to gun down the killers of his old partner here and now, began to yammer:

'I wasn't in on it, either, Callender. I just came into the café with Galliver.'

'I know you weren't in on it, Askew,' retorted Will coldly. 'I've seen Lone-Star's body – and there were no bullets in his back! But I figure you an' Galliver need a lesson for allowin' this kind of killin' in the town where you're supposed to keep the peace.'

There was a hard, humour-lacking grin on Will Callender's face as he waved Askew back against the wall with a motion of a gun.

Standing behind the counter, Stella Rivers felt a cold qualm of fear seep through her. Was this strange paradox of a man, so mild on occasion and yet so obviously one of the gun-hung border breed, about to shoot down his enemies here in her uncle's café?

The Tambaugh gunmen, Gifford and le Platte

clutching their wounds, stood wide-eyed against the wall. Each remembered with fearsome apprehension that this man had sized them up before destroying the mine-shaft at Silica Ridge. Sized them up with cold eyes and took note of their names – marking them down for death.

They waited; fearsomely, silently.

'You can relax,' Callender told them, with that cold grin. 'I'm not going to kill you now, that's not my style.' He turned to where Jake Kurdia cowered:

'Kurdia, open the door and walk out. The rest of you follow him and stand in line on the sidewalk. Pass through the door in single file and don't risk any tricks.'

Jake Kurdia limped to the door, threw it open and walked out. The miners from Silica Ridge trooped after the café proprietor, followed by Callender, guns levelled upon them.

Outside they dutifully stood in line against the clapboard wall of the café. With his guns trained on the miners, Callender nodded to the five horses hitched at the rack with his palomino.

'Kurdia, take the rifles out of the saddle-scabbards on those cayuses,' he ordered. 'Throw them well out into the middle of the street. Don't try to pull a trigger while you handle them, or you'll be dead meat before you hit the dust!'

Stella Rivers, watching through the window, saw her uncle obey the command. He pitched each of the Winchesters out into the centre of the street. In spite of the fact that the distant gates of dawn were now beginning to open and the sky was flushing with the first light of a new day, townsfolk who had been kept from their beds by the ferocity of that night were beginning to group around Kurdia's café. They stood watching the tableau enacted on the sidewalk, keeping at respectful distances.

Callender walked towards the man who now called himself Roy Collis. With a swift action he ripped the marshal's star from his black, square-cut coat, still keeping a hold on the Colt with the hand which divested the Arizona back-shooter of his authority as a lawman. He moved to Clay Galliver and tore his deputy's badge from his shirt with the same contemptuous action.

'You can't do this!' mouthed Lafe Askew in indignation. 'We're elected peace officers!'

'I've done it,' answered Callender. 'As for you bein' elected peace officers, you were elected by one man – Cy Tambaugh. He put you in charge of his kind of law in his town because you rode into this territory with spotty gun reputations. I don't think much of peace officers who are elected by one big *hombre* holding a whip in his hand, but since that seems to be the custom around here I'm electin' a new marshal for Crimson Peak. I'm electin' me, Lafe. I figure I'm a better lawman than a greasy little polecat with a back-shootin' reputation.'

The folk of Crimson Peak, intrigued by this deprivation of the peace officers' authority, gathered nearer the boardwalk, watching the tall man from Arizona. From his tight lips came a curt order:

'Mount up, all of you,' Will commanded. The Tambaugh men, a little puzzledly, obeyed and climbed into the saddles of the horses, with Will's Colts trained unwaveringly upon them.

'Now ride!' snapped Will Callender. 'Ride south and keep ridin'. Don't make for Silica Ridge an' don't swing about an' make for Tambaugh's ranch. Keep ridin' for Mexico an' stay south of the border. Don't ever come back this way – if you do, I'll kill you on sight!'

'You can't do it,' protested the slim youngster called Milt Walker. 'You can't do it, Callender. Three of these guys are wounded. It's desert country from here to the border an' we have no water in our canteens!'

Will Callender stood motionless and bleak-faced. The unwavering Colts lined on the group of mounted men.

'I don't give a damn, kid,' he replied in a colourless voice. 'I'm givin' you a chance to live – I'm givin' you a far better chance than my brother had when you *hombres* murdered him in his bunk an' a better chance than the old-timer had, even though he gave you a handful of hell before you killed him! You stand a good chance of surviving the desert an' you should make San Geronimo in Mexico in about a day an' a half of steady ridin'. Now, all of you, unholster your artillery an' drop 'em in the dirt. Make it pronto with no tricks!'

The surly Tambaugh men pulled their guns from leather slowly. The threat of the levelled Colts held by the grimfaced Callender was too great for any of them to attempt firing on him. The weapons thudded heavily into the dust at the horses' hooves.

The youthful Clay Galliver leaned forward in his saddle. His thin lips were drawn across his prominent teeth in a snarl.

'I'll come back an' kill you, Callender,' he growled.

'I've heard you say that before, Galliver,' responded Will. 'Like I just told you, I'll shoot you down on sight if you show up around here again.'

'Make sure I don't come back an' see you first – without you catchin' sight of me,' answered the wounded ex-deputy marshal.

Will eyed him with icy orbs in which needle-points of light glimmered dangerously.

'I'll remember that you've been hobnobbin' with the meanest an' yellowest back-shooter ever to owlhoot it out of Arizona Territory, Galliver – and I'll be on my guard accordingly. Now ride! Ride for Mexico or die on the desert!'

The Arizonan raised a Colt and blasted the early morning air with two crashing shots. The five mounted men were bucked in their saddles as the horses leapt at the sound of the barking six-gun. Gifford and la Platte slumping in the saddles, the mounted party moved out of town watched by Callender, standing spread-legged in the street with guns still levelled; Stella Rivers at the café window; Jake Kurdia on the plank-walk and the knot of inquisitive citizenry of Crimson Peak.

Once, before they disappeared around the high
structure of Seth Rittendon's livery stable, Clay
Galliver turned about in his saddle and bestowed a
hard glance on the man who had elected himself
marshal of the town.

Will turned to Kurdia.

'Go inside, Kurdia. Don't let me find you layin' a
hand on your niece again. Go to bed an' don't make
any attempt to sneak out to the CT outfit to tell
Tambaugh of developments here!' As Kurdia was
making his disgruntled way to the door of the café,
Will added: 'Tell Miss Rivers to come to the
marshal's office in the morning.'

Holstering his Colts, he walked towards the dead
form of Ed Costain and turned the corpse over with
his toe. He surveyed the body and that of obese Chet
Conners for some two minutes, then realized that a
small man with a gloomy face adorned with a whiskey-
reddened nose had detached himself from the knot
of watching people and was standing at his side.

'I'm Elijah Tonks, the local undertaker, marshal,'
he announced in tones suited to his calling. 'Shall I
plant these men in Boot Hill?'

'These two can go to Boot Hill,' responded Will.
'The ole-timer near the hotel is worth somethin'
better. Where do you bury the decent folk of the
town?'

'In back of the Meetin' House up the street
apiece. The Meetin' House has been unused since
the Reverend Rivers died, but we still bury the dead
in the plot at the back of it.'

Will nodded, wondering absently what kin the late Reverend Rivers was to Stella.

'Take care of these two; I'll look after the old man,' he told the undertaker. He crossed to where his old trail-partner lay and picked up the limp form tenderly. As though the watching citizenry did not exist he carried the corpse of Lone-Star Dobbins in the direction of the clapboard Meeting House that Elijah Tonks had indicated.

At the rear of the building, evidently erected by someone – no doubt the Reverend Rivers – in an attempt to bring some formal religion to this rugged land, he found the burial plot. It was dotted with wooden markers, denoting the resting places of those considered worthy of a grave in a better spot than Boot Hill, where the gun-hung flotsam without kith or kin were buried.

To one side of the plot he found a wooden shack in which there were shovels and a number of plain wooden markers.

Callender worked for an hour and a half behind the Meeting House. When he trudged away in the light of the first rays of another day's blaze of sunshine, he left a new marker planted in the earth. On it, lettered with a stub of pencil, was the legend:

'George Dobbins, of Texas. Sometime a gallant soldier in the cause of the Confederate States of America and for many years a zealous and coura-geous officer in the Arizona Territorial Rangers. Died while defending his life against assassins.'

Some day, Will promised himself, he would raise

something more lasting than a wooden marker over Lone-Star's grave.

The star of the town marshal was glittering on Will Callender's vest as he walked towards the office of that functionary and there was a certain grim humour in his wearing the emblem that did not fail to appeal to the big Arizonan. Here he was in Tambaugh's town, filling the boots of a Tambaugh man.

There was relish to be found in speculating how Cy Tambaugh would react to this move of the audacious gunslinger who came to openly defy his sway in this territory.

But there was also danger. This was a place in which almost everyone and everything was owned by Cy Tambaugh. There might well be someone who would attempt to put a bullet in his back from the cover of some night-shrouded alleyway or door; someone who would attempt to kill him in his sleep or someone who would try to remove him by sniping from a distance with a Winchester. He was in Tambaugh's town, wearing Tambaugh's star, and ready to deal out law and order the fair and square way, as he had done in the Arizona Rangers. But he would have to move like a man walking on eggs.

He found that the law-office was a square building of sun-whitened adobe bricks standing halfway along the town's single street. Standing up from its flat roof, flush with the front of the building, was a board on which letters of peeling paint spelled out:

'Town Marshal. Crimson Peak.'

Will reproached himself at first when he recalled that he had failed to relieve Lafe Askew of the keys to the office, but he found the door of the marshal's office unlocked.

It was of a pattern usual for such official buildings throughout the south-west. The stuffy front office contained a spur-scuffed desk and a couple of rickety chairs. The usual bundle of reward dodgers gathered dust on a nail in the wall. A smile quirked Will's lips as he reflected that 'Marshal Roy Collis' would no doubt have made certain that no such dodgers for Lafe Askew, issued by Sheriff John Behan of Cochise County, Arizona, would be among that bundle.

An assortment of rifles was stacked in a rack in one corner. A scuffed old saddle was thrown untidily in a corner; a couple of pairs of handcuffs and an old gunbelt, empty holstered and in an advanced stage of dry-rot, depended from a peg on another wall. In a gloomy corner stood a stove with a rust-eaten pipe canted at a crazy angle. It looked as though neither Askew nor Galliver were notably house-proud. Dust lay thick about the floor.

In a smaller compartment opening off the main office was a tiny cell, while another door opened on to a room in which there were two unmade bunks and an old washstand backed by a cracked mirror and littered with razors and the assortments of personal belongings a man gathered about him.

Will took stock of the room, noting the position

of the bunks in relation to the small window through which the sunlight speared bright shafts. He would not sleep in either. The window offered too much scope for a sniper with Tambaugh sympathies to kill a man sleeping in either of the bunks.

Callender went to the rear of the law office and found it boasted a stable in which were housed the horses of Lafe Askew and Clay Galliver. He noted that the marshal's office was flanked by a general store on the right and a barber shop on the left, both establishments separated from it by trash scattered alleys. Will wondered whether the owners of these places were Tambaugh sympathisers or otherwise, but time would tell.

Later he walked his horse from the hitch-rack outside Kurdia's and stalled the animal in the stable behind the law office. The self-elected marshal of Crimson Peak took the Winchester from his saddle scabbard, checked its magazine and placed it against the inner jamb of the office door. In the office he found a box of cartridges for one of the weapons in the rack in the corner, an old Henry rifle which appeared to be in good condition. This he loaded and placed close to the leg space of the desk.

In so doing he was putting into practice a piece of advice given him by Wyatt Earp, of Tombstone.

'Don't get caught short in a law office without a rifle or shotgun near to hand,' Earp had told him. Callender figured this advice of a famed frontier law-dog who had once held off a Tombstone mob single-handed was worth heeding.

Later he seated himself behind the desk, sitting at an angle so he could see the segment of street that was framed by the narrow door. Directly opposite was a derelict store of crumbling adobe. One or two townsfolk, out and about early, passed the door, bestowing curious glances at the man who had bucked Tambaugh to the extent of electing himself marshal of Crimson Peak. Nobody offered a greeting.

Will swung his long legs on to the scarred surface of the desk and sat in a typical town marshal's attitude, waiting, as marshals always were.

At the time Will Callender was planting the rowels of his spurs into the scuffed wood of the marshal's desk, five horses were struggling onwards, fetlock-deep in the alkali-powdered sand of the desert bottoms.

In the cloudless azure of the wide sky the white gong of the sun was climbing towards its zenith. Dave la Platte slumped in his saddle, his wounded shoulder drooping. Blood was crusted around the ugly shot wound in Wally Gifford's jaw. Young Milt Walker rode alongside these two in silence, while Lafe Askew and Clay Galliver brought up the rear.

For miles ahead, the desert floor flattened away into the purpled distance; somewhere beyond that hazed horizon lay Old Mexico.

This was a wasteland, waterless and gaunt, where distant ragged buttes reared against the blaze of the sky and the occasional saguaro cacti stood with saluting arms, often three times higher than a mounted man. It was a painted land of vivid hues, stark and fearsomely beautiful.

Lagging at the rear of the party, Galliver said: 'I'm goin' back!' The youthful ex-deputy marshal of Crimson Peak had said that a number of times since leaving the town and yet had made no move towards carrying out the action. 'We can't go on without water – we'll never get off the desert alive. By the time the sun gets full up we'll be crazy with thirst! I'm goin' back an' circlin' for Silica Ridge. The other guys there have guns. I'm gettin' one an' goin' for Callender!'

'You're talkin' like a fool,' retorted Lafe Askew. 'You've got a bum arm an' you'd never take Callender – besides, you're scared of him!'

'Scared – me?' Clay Galliver's killer's mouth was drawn back in a scornful snarl. 'I ain't so scared as you. You put your hands on the table an' held 'em there the first time Callender showed up. He called you a back-shootin' owlhooter an' you took it! I ain't scared an' my bones ain't gonna bleach on the desert. I'm goin' back to get Callender!'

'Mister Tambaugh wants him alive—' began Askew.

'I don't care about Tambaugh,' cut in Galliver. 'I'm lookin' out for myself an' I'm goin' back to fix Callender.'

'You're a fool, Galliver,' growled Wally Gifford. 'Callender's given us a chance to get out from under with a whole skin. He could have killed us for gunnin' down the ole-timer!'

'Sure,' put in young Milt Walker, 'he could have killed us, but he gave us a chance to ride out.'

'You're scared too,' scorned Galliver, 'but then you always were a lily-white choirboy! They tell me you heaved your guts up after Bob Callender was ventilated, an' you sure didn't distinguish yourself any in the fight with the ole galoot back there!'

Under the brim of his Stetson Walker's lean young face set into hard planes as he glowered at the buck-toothed young gunman.

'What about you, la Platte?' queried Galliver. 'Are you scared too? Is the big-shot border gunnie runnin' for Mexico because he's got a slug in his leg an' another in his shoulder?'

Dave la Platte, slumped in the saddle, gave the jeering youngster an ugly glance.

'Sure,' he answered. 'Callender gave us a break an' I'm gettin' out!'

'Gettin' out,' mimicked Clay Galliver. 'Gettin' out with your guilty consciences – tryin' to put the killin' of Bob Callender an' the shootin' of ole Peg-leg behind you, eh? You're lettin' yourselves be taken by one guy who comes along throwin' his weight around. Well, I'm goin' back to fix him! You ain't gonna see my bones crumblin' in the alkali dust.'

'Why don't you go back instead of talkin' about it?' demanded Wally Gifford, his wounded jaw causing him to speak with difficulty.

'Sure! Sure, I'm goin' back!' retorted Clay Galliver with a high-pitched laugh of bravado. 'I'm goin' back to Silica Ridge to get me a gun. Then I'm goin' after Callender, whether Tambaugh wants him alive or not!'

He wheeled his mount in a sudden flurry of white dust. The remaining four, twisted about in their saddles, watched his dusty back-trail plume away in the direction they had come as he tried to urge some speed out of the desert-wearied mount.

Even border ruffians of the type of Askew, la Platte and Gifford had their peculiar code of honour, however tainted with selfishness. They had been in on the brutal murder of a man's brother and his friend. That man had held them under the mouths of two guns and could have shot them down with ease; instead, he had given them a chance to clear out with their lives with the threat that he would kill them on sight if they were to cross his trail again.

It was a good enough bargain for men of their stamp. After all, they could easily have been as dead as Chet Conners and Ed Costain at this very moment! A good enough bargain for all except Clay Galliver. He was now raising a distant dust-plume in the direction of Silica Ridge.

It was an incident that was to have repercussions.

# EIGHT

Stella Rivers stepped into the law office when the golden sunshine of the forenoon was gilding Crimson Peak's shabby street.

The girl was no longer wearing the stained overall she had on when Will had seen her on the two previous occasions. Her worn dress of simple pattern was made of calico, its 'leg-of-mutton' sleeves being the only concession made to the fashionable feminine garb of the period. A cameo locket was clipped at the high gathered collar circling her slender throat. Her jet-black hair had been carefully brushed back into a smooth sweep down her back and tied with a ribbon.

As she entered the door, with the sunlight touching out the signs of strain on her pale, delicately-moulded features, Callender felt he had never seen so lovely a young woman, not even among the bevies of youthful beauties he had mingled with in those Chicago days which now seemed so long distant.

89

He swung his legs from the desk as the girl entered, stood upright and doffed his hat.

' 'Mornin', ma'am,' he greeted, indicating a chair.

'Good morning, Mr Callender. My uncle said you wanted to see me this morning.' She said the words cautiously, and Callender again noted the cultured edge to her speech.

'An' he didn't go runnin' to Tambaugh's outfit,' mused Will aloud. 'Your Uncle Jake is gettin' to be a right good boy, Miss Rivers. I guess we'll have to send him to the head of the class.'

'My uncle is frightened of you, Mr Callender,' she replied simply. 'What did you want me for?'

'I've elected myself peace officer here, Miss Rivers, as you know. I did that because I knew the men who were supposed to fill that capacity enforced no law but Cy Tambaugh's. When I tell you, in confidence, that I was a captain in the Arizona Rangers before coming here, perhaps you at least will have some faith in my powers as a lawman. I heard enough before I busted into the café last night to gather that you shouted a warning to old Lone-Star Dobbins and gave him a chance to fight back.'

The girl nodded, biting her lip.

'They were going to shoot him in the back,' she said with a quaver in her voice, 'an old cripple like him!'

'Lone-Star was no cripple with his guns, as I guess you noticed. I'm grateful to you for givin' him a chance to draw. He and I were very old friends. I want you to make a statement of what happened last night, since you're about the only person in this town I care to trust as well as being a witness to the gunfight. I then intend to keep the statement on the off-chance that I can use it in evidence if I ever get the wheels of the law turning against Tambaugh and his hawks.'

'Will it mean incriminating Uncle Jake?'

'Not unless he was in on the shootin' an' I noticed he wasn't carrying a gun last night. You just tell me the truth. I'll write it down an' you can sign it. If ever a case comes of the business, your uncle and yourself might be called to give evidence.'

'Very well,' Stella agreed. Will opened a drawer of the desk and produced some time-yellowed sheets of legal paper. The girl told of the happenings at her uncle's restaurant the previous night, watching him write her words down in an educated Spencerian hand so unbefitting to his border drifter's dress.

When he had finished taking the dictation, Will handed the raven-haired girl the paper. She read it and signed it. Callender took the statement and placed it in the drawer of the desk.

'I don't go in for askin' people their business as a rule,' he told Stella, 'but how come you have such feelin' for your uncle? He treats you the way I would-n't treat an Injun hound-dog.'

'For my mother's sake, I guess. He's her brother – she's dead now – and he was different before he was crippled by a crazy steer one day on the CT round-up. He became bitter and surly after the accident.'

'So Kurdia was a Tambaugh rider?' queried Will.

'Yes, he was the CT strawboss for some years.'

'And he's the only kin you have?'

'He's all I have left since my father died. He was pastor here when there were signs of Crimson Peak becoming a thriving settlement. It didn't, and Tambaugh came along to get his hands on this section of the territory. I was at school in St Louis, but I had to come back after my father died. I hoped I might teach school out here, but there weren't enough children and there was no schoolhouse. I made an attempt to start a little school for the few children in the town, using Daddy's old Meeting House. But it didn't work out and I finished up keeping house for Uncle Jake.'

Will Callender rose and stood behind the slight seated figure of the girl. He put a hand on her shoulder and there was something protective about the gesture.

'Keepin' house for him,' he repeated quietly, 'an' slingin' hash in his greasy eating-house an' bein' bullied by him – all for the sake of your mother. You're a fine young lady, Miss Rivers, but you deserve something better.'

The girl half turned, looking upwards at him. He saw her swallow hard.

'Mr Callender – Will—' she faltered. 'Take care! This is a dangerous town for you. When Tambaugh finds out about you running Collis and Galliver out of town and setting yourself up as marshal he'll—'

Will silenced her, increasing his grip on her shoulder.

'Don't worry about me. I'll handle Tambaugh,' he told her.

'But take care,' she persisted. 'There are men in Crimson Peak who are wholly on Tambaugh's side. My uncle is one; he's scared of you, but there are others who might back him up and he may find the courage to act. Don't underestimate Tambaugh or his followers in this town.'

Will Callender seated himself at the desk once more.

'These Tambaugh men, who are they?' he queried. 'Who should I watch out for?'

'Seth Rittendon at the livery stable, he's one of Tambaugh's men,' answered Stella. 'Then there are Charlie Krantz, who runs the blacksmith's shop along the street; Sam Wollingham, the barber right next door. They're all Tambaugh men – all of them worked for Cy Tambaugh at one time or another.'

'And the other townsfolk?' he asked.

'The majority are on the fence, but there are a lot of Tambaugh sympathizers. Setting yourself up as marshal here in Tambaugh's town means you're an open target,' she warned.

'I know it and I'm stickin' here,' he retorted; and she caught once again that tightening of his hard features that showed him for a man who went after what he wanted and usually got it.

When Stella left the office Callender stood close to the door watching her slight figure dwindle in the direction of her uncle's restaurant. Then he turned and seated himself behind the desk once again, telling himself he would see her again when he went across to the restaurant for breakfast a little later, and still later when he went for lunch, and would see her yet again when he went for supper.

He suddenly got himself into perspective, dragged his feelings into the open and analysed them objectively.

'You damn' fool!' he told himself half aloud. 'Bringing the girl across here, taking a statement and making big talk about the law and laying up evidence against Lone-Star's killers – when you've already hazed some of the principals in the case towards the safety of Mexico! Why don't you admit to yourself that the whole thing was a subterfuge because you wanted to get to know her and something about her? Why don't you admit, you blamed half-wit, that you fell for her the moment you clapped eyes on her and knew she was your kind? Why don't you admit you're in love with her?'

The distant desert rims were touched with the ruddy finger of the setting sun when Clay Galliver urged his near-exhausted horse into the mining camp at Silica Ridge. The men who met the ex-deputy marshal of Crimson Peak were not out-and-out gunmen in the service of Tambaugh as Conners, la Platte, Gifford and Costain had been. They were merely mining for the wages paid by Tambaugh. They had no deep loyalty to the lord of this territory.

Galliver came into their midst, sloped forward in the saddle, his right arm still in its grimy sling. The gaunt horse and the hollowed eyes of the dust-peppered rider spoke of long hours in the wilderness.

'Gimme some grub an' a gun,' demanded Galliver, descending wearily from the saddle. 'Gimme some grub an' a gun, pronto! Don't stand around staring, damn you!'

'What's happened?' asked one of the miners. 'Where's Conners an' la Platte an' the others?'

Galliver began to leg his weary way towards the cook-shack.

'Dead, that's where Conners is – an' Costain. We jumped that peg-legged oldster in town an' he got them before we got him. Then Callender showed up an' ran the rest of us out of town. He said he was takin' over as marshal an' he hazed la Platte, Gifford, Walker, Collis an' me off over the desert. Told us to ride for the border an' either get there or die on the desert. I went so far an' no further. I'm goin' back to get Callender. I guess the other fools are buzzard meat by now. They were all yellow. Said they'd had enough an' went for Mexico without a word.'

Clay Galliver began to help himself to food in the cook-shack. Someone produced hot coffee for him and the miners gathered around him to hear the story of the gunfight in Crimson Peak.

They were men who had drifted into the mine since Cy Tambaugh had claimed it by his well-laid plan. They had been aware, with the deep superstition of miners, that the mine was 'bad', as had old

Lone-Star Dobbins, who had not been the first to roll his blankets and ride out of Silica Ridge. Unlike those who had ridden out with Chet Conners, they had not taken part in the killing of the original owner of the silver strike. Indeed, none of these men knew how Tambaugh had come by the Silica Ridge mine, for Chet Conners and his gun-hung companions had always remained tight-lipped about the killing of the 'bank-robber' in the cabin – a silence for which Cy Tambaugh paid good money.

Nevertheless, the miners, although they were mostly of the solitary desert-rat type who usually shunned towns, had heard ugly rumours drifting around. They were stories that rankled, stories of how Cy Tambaugh had gradually taken the reins into his iron grip where the running of this land was concerned. Stories of nesters hustled off their narrow-hoed corn patches at gun-point. Stories of men who tried to make their own way and wound up either moulded into Tambaugh's service or lying bullet-pounded in some lonely dry-wash.

Then there was the tall, bleak-eyed man who had blown up the mine shaft so recently. He had spoken of his brother being killed by a party of Tambaugh riders here at Silica Ridge. This suggestion of another ugly story, enacted on their very doorstep, planted a dark, suspicious foreboding in their distrustful desert men's minds.

They listened to Clay Galliver's wild talk of riding back to Crimson Peak to kill the self-elected marshal. To a man they decided they would ride in search of other jobs. Whatever had been building up between Tambaugh and the grey-eyed gun-packer who had blown up the mine shaft now seemed to be coming to a head. They wanted no part of someone else's bullet trouble.

At approximately the same time Galliver reached Silica Ridge, another group of men were listening to another sweat-streaked rider who had pounded into the headquarters of the CT ranch on a lathered mount. He was Seth Rittendon, the liveryman from Crimson Peak. He now stood in the yard fronting the ranch-house, situated on the rolling rangeland far to the north of the town. Cy Tambaugh, his brow black as thunder, as well as a crowd of CT wranglers, hard-faced men sporting much hardware, listened to Rittendon.

'. . . then he ran 'em all out of town. Told 'em he'd shoot 'em on sight if they came back,' gabbled the little liveryman. 'Put Collis's star on his vest an' said he figured he could run the law in Crimson Peak better than Collis an' Galliver.'

'Why didn't I learn of this sooner?' thundered Cy Tambaugh. 'Callender's been strutting around Crimson Peak wearing my star all day and you come out here at night to tell me!'

'I had to watch my chance, Mister Tambaugh,' quavered Seth Rittendon. 'He's been watchin' the street all day – watchin' like a hawk. An' someone's put him wise to me an' Krantz an' Wollingham bein' on your side an' he watched us every time we showed ourselves on the street. He just sat on the gallery of the marshal's office watchin' the street. He sat there all day 'cept for when he was eating at Kurdia's. I had to watch my chance to slip out of town – I didn't want any of his slugs in me!'

'You say he's wise as to where the sympathies of yourself, Krantz and Wollingham lie? Who put him wise?' questioned Tambaugh.

'I think it was that niece of Kurdia's. I was watching from the stable this mornin' an' saw her go across to the marshal's office. She was in there a long time – they must have had quite a pow-wow.'

A smouldering light of evil glowed in Cy Tambaugh's eyes and he rubbed a heavily-ringed hand over his flabby face thoughtfully.

'So Stella Rivers is hob-nobbing with Callender,' he mused. 'I guess she would at that; she has the same sense of values as her stupid, preaching father. She'd figure Callender for an upstanding law-and-order man!'

A tall rider, with the long features of a Mexican, nudged his gun loose in its leather impatiently. 'Why don't we ride in an' fix this *hombre's* wagon right now?' he growled.

'We'll ride in, Chavez,' retorted Tambaugh, 'but we'll fix Will Callender my way. I want him alive, remember. At least until I have some information out of him.'

'Information!' scorned Mex Chavez, curling his lips over shiny white teeth. 'Why don't we ride in an' kill him? We heard all about what he's supposed to be holdin' over you. Forget it, Mister Tambaugh.

Information about some fool woman—'

Cy Tambaugh stepped forward and smote a stinging, open-handed slap across Mex Chavez's mouth,
killing the sentence on his lips. His eyes were now
smouldering dangerously. He stood facing Chavez in
the gloom, every inch of his grey-clad body quivering with rage and his knuckles bunched.

'Don't let me ever hear you talk like that again,
Chavez,' he hissed, breathing heavily. 'You forget
who's in the saddle around here! I'm giving the
orders! Callender is going to be taken alive, and he
stays alive until I say otherwise. My offer of a reward
still goes. The man who takes him with a whole skin
gets enough coin to keep his pants pockets jingling
for a long time – that should be good enough for
you *hombres*!'

Mex Chavez rubbed his mouth ruefully. 'Sorry,
Mister Tambaugh,' he said penitently.

'Keep your tongues in your mouth in future,'
commanded Cy Tambaugh. 'Now, all of you – get
some slugs in your guns and saddle up!'

# NINE

Will Callender settled down for the first night of his tenure of office as marshal of Crimson Peak.

In the darkness he allowed himself a smile of satisfaction. There had been something gratifying in being posted as a wanted man in Tambaugh's territory and openly walking the cattle baron's town with the star of peace officer on his vest. Not that Will allowed himself any illusions as to his safety – which was why he chose the sleeping place into which he was now settling.

He was on the flat, adobe roof of the law office, immediately behind the board which fronted the street with the designation of the office painted upon it. Behind that board, lying flat as he was, he was invisible to anyone on the street. He had approached this position by climbing the rear of the building, bringing with him a blanket from the sleeping quarters of the law office. He would have preferred his own bedroll, but this was still in the

camp outside town which he left in hasty pursuit of
Lone-Star.

In one of the bunks in the sleeping quarters of
the marshal's office he had fixed a bundle of junk,
huddled under a blanket, to simulate a sleeping
figure.

It was just a hunch and it might pay off.

With his Winchester and gunbelt beside him, Will
rolled himself in the blanket and lay behind the
long length of the sign-board, using his hat as a
pillow. He lay on his back, looking at the scattered
points of the stars in the wide, dark sky. A paradox of
a wind, half warm with the heat of the desert, yet
chilled with the cool of the night, breathed across
the town.

Someone was tinkling out a mournful tune on the
jangling piano down at the Palacio. A coyote yowled
dismally somewhere on the desert rims.

Will lay awake thinking of the day he had spent
mostly watching the street of Crimson Peak. It had
been a quiet enough day. He had taken his meals at
Kurdia's, where Stella had waited upon him quietly
and Jake Kurdia watched him apprehensively. From
his seat on the gallery of the office he had seen the
distance-lessened figure of Seth Rittendon watching
him from time to time from the gloomy opening of
his livery barn at the far end of the street.

Once or twice, too, a lean and crabby-faced man
with a bald, vein-corded head had shown himself
from the door of the barber shop next to the law
office. He had looked out, taking furtive glances at

the lean, gun-hung man who sat on a backward-tilted chair with one boot-heel hooked on the rail of the porch, to bolt back into his shop when he found the flinty grey eyes turned on him.

Will had also seen a heavily-built man in a leather apron walk boldly past him with insolent eyes to spend a few minutes in a small adobe cantina a little way along the street. He had left the cantina, wiping a brawny hand across his broad lips. The big man had walked slowly past the law office again, his eyes locking with those of the man on the gallery. He finally entered the low smithy building on the opposite side of the rutted street, from whence he had issued.

Lying in his blanket on the roof of the marshal's office, Will Callender thought of them. Seth Rittendon, the liveryman; Sam Wollingham, the barber; Charlie Krantz, the blacksmith – all of them men who would bear watching!

Stella Rivers' words ran through his drowsy mind: '. . . you're an open target,' she had warned him. Cy Tambaugh wanted him alive – because of Rosalind – but there were others who might attempt to gun him down. Hence the dummy in the bunk in the office and his choice of the roof as a sleeping place.

At length the clangour of the piano down at the Palacio ceased. Even the coyote on the desert stopped his weird keening. Will was on the edge of the abyss of sleep; the street below him was silent.

It came slowly, half lost in the distance at first, but growing louder and coming nearer. The sound of a

walking horse accompanied by the jangle of trappings. Will lay open-eyed and tensed in the darkness. The sound came from the southern end of the
town, from somewhere down near the Palacio
Hotel. The sound of a man riding, faint as yet, but
definite.

It ceased.

Will rolled out of the blanket. Flat on his stomach
he slithered across the roof, keeping behind the
cover of the sign-board. He reached the edge of the
board and peered around it. He saw him in the act
of hitching his mount at the rack at the front of the
Palacio. An anonymous figure, merely a silhouette –
until he turned and the watching Arizonan saw the
arm in its sling.

'Clay Galliver!' thought Will, pressing himself
hard against the roof.

He watched the solitary figure cat-footing along
the silent street, coming in the direction of the law
office. The starlight put a sheen on the Winchester
he carried in his good left hand before he was swallowed by the shadows of the awnings over the board-
walks.

Will held his position on the roof. He could hear
Galliver approaching the building though he could
not see him. The youngster had neglected to remove
his spurs, and the tinkle of the rowels as he walked
was magnified by the silence of the sleeping town.
From his perch Callender heard the ringing of the
spurs drawing nearer. Suddenly the ex-deputy
marshal of Crimson Peak came into view, stepping

out of the shadow of the boardwalk that joined the alley running alongside the law office at right-angles.

Clay Galliver crept along the alley; above him, Will Callender edged noiselessly along the roof. Cautiously Will peered over the edge of the flat roof, looking into the alleyway.

Below him the big-hatted figure of Galliver was peering into the small window of the sleeping quarters of the marshal's office. Will watched him wield the rifle maladroitly with his uninjured left arm. He heard the sound of shattering glass as Galliver broke the window with the muzzle of the weapon.

The man in the alley positioned himself swiftly, gripping the Winchester under the armpit on his uninjured side, shoving the weapon through the hole in the window-pane and triggering it with his good hand at the dummy in the bunk.

Even as the rifle boomed into the narrow confines of the small room, Will Callender dropped from the roof.

He fell upon the man in the alley with the swiftness of a pouncing puma, landing squarely on Galliver's shoulders and crooking an arm about his neck. Galliver gave a startled yelp and collapsed under the falling weight of Callender. Both men fell to the trash-littered floor of the alley in a threshing tangle of arms and legs.

Somehow, Clay Galliver managed to roll under Callender and crook a knee upwards. He took Callender in the groin, lifting him clear with a savage thrust.

Callender snorted in pain and went sprawling into the dust. He lay there for a moment, his face in the muck, panting, trying to regain the wind that Galliver had knocked out of him. He gathered himself up and whirled about, crouching in the dust, to face the ex-deputy. He was about to spring, but he froze in his crouching position.

Galliver was only a couple of yards away, on his knees, with the Winchester levelled squarely at Callender. The starlight that struggled into the gloomy alley illuminated his shadow-darkened, Billy the Kid face, showing the buck teeth bared in a murderous leer.

Even with his one-armed method of firing, Galliver could not miss his target at this range. He fired, the bark of the rifle clattering flatly along the alleyway.

In the very face of the shot Will threw himself to one side. He was so near to Galliver's weapon that the coughing belch of muzzle-flame scorched the side of his face and the slug almost nicked his ear as it went screaming down the alley. Once more he sprawled into the filth of the alley, falling hard against the adobe wall of Sam Wollingharn's barber shop.

He rolled in the shadows telling himself he was a fool. Both his six-guns and his Winchester were on the roof of the law office. He had figured Galliver would be easy meat and had dropped on him weaponless. He had figured wrongly; he faced Galliver in a tiny alley with nothing but his bare hands, while Galliver still had the Winchester.

The terse, quick click of another shell being pumped into the Winchester caused him to look up.

Through the drifting veil of gunsmoke he saw Clay Galliver, standing now. He had backed a few paces down the alley to give himself distance for the shot. He had the rifle gripped tight against his body, its mouth pointed directly at the crouching Callender.

He was grinning again. Taking his time. Relishing it.

It was going to be so easy!

Crouching on the ground, Callender tensed, watching the face of the man who was preparing to kill him, grinning through the acrid-smelling cordite smoke.

His hand suddenly contacted something hard and sharp lying in the dirt of the alley. It was a broken bottle. He grabbed it and hurled it at Galliver with all the force he could muster, then flung himself across the alley, to sprawl against the wall of the marshal's office.

The bottle smote Clay Galliver on the jaw at the very instant he triggered the Winchester. Galliver grunted and went reeling against the adobe wall of the law office as his rifle spat white flame and the slug kicked up a spout of dirt at Will Callender's feet.

Will picked himself up. He heard his adversary curse in the swirl of gunsmoke that filled the narrow alley. The sound of another round being pumped into the Winchester came.

Callender turned and went haring down the alley

in the direction of the street. As he turned the corner of the marshal's office, gaining the board-walk, the Winchester bellowed behind him and dry adobe spurted as the bullet sliced the corner of the wall inches above his head. He pounded along the plank-walk, lurched against the door of the law office, shouldering it open.

He ran, half-crouching, into the gloom of the office. Out on the plank-walk the pounding of Galliver's pursuing feet and the jangle of his spurs sounded close.

In the darkened office Will stumbled towards the desk and groped behind it for the single-shot Henry that he had placed close to the knee aperture.

He grabbed the weapon and whirled, cat-like, facing the door. Clay Galliver appeared, standing on the boardwalk, framed in the doorway and looking into the dark office.

'I'm in here, Galliver!' roared Callender.

The youngster tried to throw the muzzle of his rifle in the direction of the voice, and Callender let drive with the old Henry. The shot bellowed out of the blackness in a jagged blossom of flame. Clay Galliver scooted back on his heels the entire width of the plank sidewalk and flopped over backwards into the dust of the street.

Callender, still carrying the old rifle, walked to the door through the swirl of eye-stinging smoke. He leaned his weight on the jamb, catching his breath and looking out at the lifeless form of Clay Galliver spreadeagled in the dirt.

He remembered Wyatt Earp's advice about always having a loaded rifle or shotgun planted near to hand in a law office, and reflected that he would thank Earp for that valuable tip if he ever ran across him again.

Suddenly he stiffened.

The distance-muffled sound of many horses drumming along in a solid body beset his ears. He took a quick step forward on to the boardwalk and faced the direction from which the growing hoof-thunder sounded – northwards, the direction in which lay the CT outfit's headquarters.

Where the street petered away beyond the last squat buildings of the township, a white, hoof-raised plume of alkali dust drifted upwards in the starlight.

A large body of horsemen coming – and he was standing here with an unloaded, single-shot Henry rifle!

Will flung the useless weapon into the black mouth of the office door, turned about and ran for the alleyway leading to the rear of the building. He began to scramble up the rear wall of the structure, using the protruding adobe bricks for foot and hand-holds. Up on the roof he crouched low – mindful that Kurdia, Wollingham, Krantz or Rittendon might be lurking somewhere about, attracted by the recent shooting.

He made his way to where his sleeping gear, rifle and six-guns lay, crouching as low as possible. The approaching thunder of hooves grew louder in his ears.

His cartridge-studded gunbelt buckled about him, he took up his Winchester and pumped a shell into the breech. He clutched the weapon, lying flat behind the sign-board that fronted the street. He inched his head around the end of the board so that he could see the sweep of the street, running northwards. He was in deep shadow up here and his hatless head could not be seen from below.

The staccato tramping of many hooves was growing louder and the drift of dust was nearer. Will Callender lay in the dark, waiting. Presently a bobbing cluster of mounted men came drumming into sight at the end of the street, about twenty of them, all flourishing weapons in the starlight.

Callender could see the grey-garbed figure of Cy Tambaugh riding to the fore like a cavalry commander. Hooves tramped a thundering tattoo and the dust scuffed upwards in their back-trail as the riders came into the main body of the street. From his perch Callender watched them rein up before the law office, gazing incredulously at the sight of Clay Galliver stretched in the dirt. He heard Tambaugh's voice shout:

'It's Galliver! Watch out for the doorway of the office, Callender must be in there!'

The horsemen pulled their mounts to one side so they were not in a direct line with the black mouth of the office door. Will could see they were Tambaugh's hard-case range riders, all flourishing rifles or side-arms. He heard Cy Tambaugh say: 'Remember, I want him alive!' Then the cattle baron

*Gun Feud*

bellowed: 'If you're in there, Callender, better come out with your gun up – I want to parley!'

Up on the roof Will Callender edged around the corner of the sign-board, drawing a bead on the top of Tambaugh's high-crowned Stetson with his Winchester. He fired, shattering the still air with the cracking shot. Cy Tambaugh's headgear went spinning from his head. His horse and those of his riders reared high in snorting panic at the sudden bark of the weapon.

'Get out of town – the whole bunch of you!' yelled Will, jerking the pump of the rifle.

Tambaugh, jouncing around in his saddle, fighting to quell the panicked horse and regain his composure after the unexpected shot, looked upwards.

'Don't be a fool, Callender! Come down from there and pow-wow!' he called.

'I said get out of town,' repeated Will. 'I'm lawman in this town on my own say-so. When a bunch of murderers ride into a town, a lawman either runs 'em out or kills 'em! For my money you an' your crew are murderers; I'm fixin' to run you out!'

'You're a fool! Come down and make talk!' yelled Tambaugh in answer.

'The only time I'll listen to you, Tambaugh, is when you come crawlin' to tell me about the set-up on Silica Ridge when my brother died. Not that I don't know the facts already, but I want to hear them from your own lips. That can wait – right now I'm hazin' you out!'

'Supposin' we won't be hazed out?' bellowed a blackbearded ruffian from the midst of the mounted group.

'Then you can bring on the fightin'. I came here to settle a grudge; any time you force me into gunnin' you down it'll suit me.'

'Don't be addle-headed, Callender,' cried Tambaugh. 'If you try to make a fight you won't stand a chance.'

'I'll stand a better chance than my brother. I'm not lyin' asleep in a cabin, Tambaugh – I'm wide-awake with a Winchester an' two Colts.'

A long-faced rider, in garb compounded of a mixture of formal cattle-range dress and the flamboyant trappings of a Mexican vaquero, waved a pistol and shifted uneasily in his saddle.

'Let's quit this talk. Let's act!' he bawled. 'I can see him from here – I can plug him!'

'No!' yipped Tambaugh urgently. 'I want Callender alive!'

'The hell with that kind of talk,' jeered Mex Chavez. 'We've heard enough of that stuff.'

Chavez threw his gun up towards Will's face in defiance of Tambaugh. A split second before he triggered a shot at the man on the roof, Callender fired the Winchester. Both blasts mingled into one and Will heard the plunk of Chavez's slug driving into the sign-board only a couple of inches from his ear. In the same instant Mex Chavez stiffened and stood up, full-length, in the stirrups. He pitched over backwards with an expression of surprise on his face and a hole in the centre of his forehead.

The cluster of horses down on the street began to surge about in a boiling, dust-stirring panic. Will Callender activated the loading lever of his rifle.

'All right, Tambaugh,' he bellowed huskily. 'If you want shootin', let's get to business – or clear out of town!'

# TEN

In that panicked moment Will Callender realized that the shooting of Mex Chavez had thrown no little scare into the bunch of horsemen. Wild, gunfighting, vengeance-thirsty temper was in him now and he was ready to fight it out with Tambaugh and his men to the bitter end.

Then he saw that the riders were bunching about in a flurry of dust. With Cy Tambaugh in the lead they were wheeling and hazing away from the law office, heading southward down the street. He yipped like a drunken cowpoke and loosed another Winchester shell after them. A hat was plucked out of the mass of bobbing riders, to go spinning into the dirt of the street.

Tambaugh gained sufficient control of the scared riders to halt them close to Kurdia's establishment. They whirled about in a bunch, standing in the centre of the street. Tambaugh forced his mount to the front of the knot of mounted men.

113

'You'd best come down and talk turkey if you know what's good for you, Callender,' he roared along the shadowed street.

'I said let's get to business, Tambaugh!' retorted Will from his perch. 'Either fight or keep ridin'. What's wrong with your *hombres* – are they too mannerly to fire on anyone but sleepin' youngsters an' crippled ole-timers?'

From the shadows of the awnings over the sidewalk two figures broke loose and joined the bunch of standing riders. Callender caught only the slightest glimpse of them as they crossed the street to be swallowed by the clustered mass of riders. By their build they looked like Sam Wollingham, the barber, and Charlie Krantz, the powerful smith.

Will strained his eyes along the darkened street in an attempt to see what was going on among the now silent bunch of mounted men. The silence was too ominous, but he could make out nothing of what was happening in that shadowy cluster of men and horses.

A terse conversation was in fact in progress.

'You still want him alive?' asked Charlie Krantz, now minus his leather apron.

'I want him alive and able to talk sense for ten minutes,' snorted Cy Tambaugh.

'That offer of a reward still go for the man who brings him?' asked the hefty blacksmith.

'It still goes.'

'I'll get him,' the smith informed Tambaugh. He flexed a huge muscle in his brawny arm. 'Keep him facin' the street an' I'll get him!'

The blacksmith slipped into an alleyway on the same side of the street as the marshal's office and began to make swift progress in the direction of the office, using the devious alleys at the rear of the buildings.

Cy Tamburgh and his riders held their ground. Tambaugh made a bid to keep Callender talking.

'Show some horse-sense, Callender. Come down and make talk,' he yelled.

Will answered with a harsh jeer: 'Change your tune, Tambaugh. I'm plumb sick of that same old dirge.'

'You're a damn' fool – you're up to your neck in trouble and you don't stand a chance.' the cattle baron shouted back along the street.

Callender was about to reply when a slight scraping sound behind him caused him to jerk a glance over his shoulder. A hulking figure was in the act of clambering on to the roof, his massive shoulders rearing up against the star-flecked sky. Callender, lying on his stomach, rolled over and scrambled into a crouch as the man gained the roof.

The hefty figure lumbered forward. In the frosty gleam of the stars the Arizonan caught a glimpse of the broadlipped, smouldering-eyed features of Charlie Krantz. Will clubbed the Winchester and crouched.

'I'm takin' you down, boy,' breathed the giant blacksmith.

Then he lurched forward, driving out with a brawny bunched fist.

Will thrust himself to one side in time to avoid the full force of the punch, but taking a glancing blow on the side of the jaw which sent him reeling across the roof. He staggered, regained his balance and was aware of the huge figure bearing down on him. He swung out with the clubbed rifle, landing an ineffective swipe across Krantz's shoulders.

Charlie Krantz chuckled in the gloom as the butt of the weapon bounced off him. He slammed a meaty blow on to Callender's nose. A red wash of pain welled before Callender's eyes and he went down to the coarse, adobe surface of the roof. The Winchester slipped from his grip and was lost in the darkness.

Through a haze of tears Will saw the big figure rear against the stars and come lunging forward again. Somehow he managed to coil his legs under him. He waited for the giant to take a couple of steps nearer; then, snorting blood, he drove forward in a headlong thrust, forcing himself up from the roof with all the power of his legs. The Arizonan's head smote the blacksmith in the midriff. With a gasping bellow, Charlie Krantz scuttered backwards on his heels, the wind driven out of his big frame.

Will Callender staggered forward, following up the blacksmith. Krantz had scooted back against the sign-board that stood flush with the front wall of the adobe building. He was leaning on the board, gasping for breath. Callender, still half dazed, went barging towards him, fists flailing. He handed Krantz a fist of hard knuckles, catching his eye, and followed the blow with a stinging swipe across the mouth.

Charlie Krantz lurched against the board heavily. He snorted like a wounded animal then came lumbering towards his adversary, arms akimbo, bear-like. He grabbed Will around his lean waist with a pair of huge hands. Callender could feel the powerful fingers of the giant gouging into his flesh.

He managed to crook a knee and lift it with a forceful thrust against Krantz's stomach. Krantz released his grip and went gyrating away with a gurgle of breathless pain. Hitting the sign-board, which creaked drily under the hard impact of the heavy body, he rebounded off it and stood shaking his head like a stunned ox.

Callender followed through, leaping forward like a wild thing. He looped a cracking haymaker to the giant's stubbled jaw. Krantz gave a squawk which changed into a hoarse scream as he hit the board again and it shivered from its mooring with a sharp crack. Krantz plunged backwards off the roof, arms flung wide and mouth open.

Will, standing wide-legged on the edge of the roof, saw him hit the sun-warped awning, slither down it and sprawl in the dirt of the street close to the body of Clay Galliver. He lay quite still.

Callender, struggling for breath, cast a glance southward to where Tambaugh and his party sat their horses in silence. Dawn was sliding up the wide vista of the sky. A red, raw dawn.

Callender felt that surge of fury boiling up within him again – now ten times more possessive. He stood on the roof watching the silent group of riders while they sat their mounts, along the street, immobile as so many equestrian statues.

The concept of his brother, butchered in his bunk by Tambaugh riders, followed by the memory of Lone-Star Dobbins lying bullet-pounded in the dirt, were impinged upon his consciousness. A lusting for vengeance gripped his whole being.

The big Arizonan suddenly ceased to be a spread-legged panting silhouette against the backdrop of the dawn-flushed sky. He leapt into panther-like action, jumping from the roof to the awning over the sidewalk six feet below. He slithered down the slant of the sun-bent wooden awning, half crouching, then flung himself down into the street.

By the time his boots touched dirt his guns were drawn and he was facing the group of standing riders. He stood in the centre of the street holding the pose of a gunfighter: body crouched forward, legs astride and knees slightly bent. He was a ferocious, half-wild figure with hair tousled on his hatless head and the mingled filth of the alley and blood from his punished nose plastered on his face.

He saw the grey-suited figure of Tambaugh standing out in his vision while the remaining riders seemed to fade into a haze. The memories of Bob and Lone-Star surged up in Callender's mind again.

'I told you to ride or fight!' He bellowed the words down the street in a hoarse and broken voice. 'Now I'm bringin' on the trouble, Tambaugh – I'm comin' for you, personally!'

Even across the yards separating the Tambaugh men from the wild gun-prodding creature in the middle of the street, Cy Tambaugh could see the intent in the blazing grey eyes. He wheeled his horse in a swift, spur-plunging action and made for the centre of the bunch of riders.

Callender sent a wild bullet whining after the retreating man. It missed Tambaugh as he was lost in the swirl of jostling horses, but somebody in the bunch yipped out a squawk of pain. Will saw a rider come thrusting to the fore with one hand clapped over an ear and the other flourishing a Winchester.

Will began to hare for the sidewalk on the opposite side of the street as he saw the rifle levelled. Its crack shattered up to the raw, dawn-washed sky and a spurt of dust spouted up as the slug splatted into the ground only inches from the feet of the running man.

Callender made the sidewalk. There was a shadowed merchandise store here, with boxes and kegs piled outside. Even in the act of flinging himself behind a packing-case, he heard Tambaugh's voice bleating something about wanting him alive. The rider with the Winchester rasped back: 'The hell with takin' him alive! He got Mex Chavez an' I ain't gonna sit here an' let him get me!'

Somebody else added loud agreement, and another bullet came screaming. It whanged off an upright of the store's gallery. Will triggered a couple of shots into the midst of the mounted men. Someone yipped and Will threw himself flat to the

rough planing of the sidewalk as a fusillade of angry
shots came whistling across the front of the store.

He peeked gingerly around the edge of the pack-
ing case, could see the riders broiling about in a dust
flurry. Cy Tambaugh was lost somewhere in their
midst.

Tambaugh seemed to have lost control of his
men, for a small bunch of riders was detaching itself
from the larger body, to drum along the street in the
direction of Callender's place of cover. Will was
busily thumbing cartridges from the loops at his belt
into the empty chambers of his guns. He snapped
the cylinders back into position just as the mounted
party of half a dozen whooping men came thundering level with the store.

From their saddles they peppered the gallery of
the store with a ragged scatter of whizzing shots. Will
flattened himself to the grimy boards, the bullets
whanging over his head to go spanging into the dry
wood of the building and shatter the glass of a
window.

He raised himself from the boards uninjured,
took a quick glance around the edge of the case, a
gun at the ready. The riders were in the act of wheeling about some little distance from the store,
preparing for another dash past Callender's place of
cover. They were trying Indian tactics, riding back
and forth showering their victim with shots. It was
spectacular and unnerving, but not an accurate
method of hitting a man in cover.

Will was ready for them when they came galloping

past a second time. He got the first shot in, dropping their leader, the fellow with the Winchester.

Callender blazed another couple of shots into the blurred body of horsemen and ducked quickly as their answering volley came slashing towards the gallery of the store. As he hit the boards he felt the red-hot drive of a bullet slicing into the upper part of his left arm. He cursed against clenched teeth and triggered whining lead after the retreating CT riders.

The slugs hummed harmlessly away into the shadows across the street as the Tambaugh riders put distance between themselves and the wild-eyed gunman on the gallery of the store.

Grunting with the stinging pain of his bullet-slashed arm, Will leaned against the wall of the store and took a cautious look along the street. The small group of riders had now joined the remainder of the CT bunch and some sort of activity was going on around the entrance to Kurdia's café. A number of Tambaugh's men had dismounted and were milling about the door of the eating-house.

Callender fired a blast of wild shots into their midst with a raucous Rebel yell, to be rewarded by the sound of someone hooting in anguish.

'Where's Tambaugh?' roared the big Arizonan from his cover. 'Why don't he come out an' fight?'

Then out of the midst of the crowding CT riders on the plank-walk fronting Kurdia's place came a sound that chilled Callender to the marrow – the shrill screech of a woman. He saw the crowd of men part and the grey-garbed figure of Cy Tambaugh came out on to the street. He was clutching Stella Rivers, a shawl over her nightdress, holding her by an arm crooked about her slender neck. Tambaugh was forcing the girl through the group of CT men, facing Will Callender's place of cover, so that his body was shielded by hers.

'Better throw your guns down and come over here, Callender,' the cattle baron shouted triumphantly. 'I've got a gun in this girl's back! Rumour has it you and she are friendly – better do as I say if you don't want to see her shot.'

Stella, white-faced, was struggling against the grip of the rancher. 'No, Will,' she shrilled. 'Keep fighting them – don't mind about me!'

Callender cursed behind the cover of the packing-case. So they'd busted into Kurdia's and taken the girl from her bed! If Tambaugh really had a gun at her back he might use it if he continued to resist – there was no telling with a snake like Tambaugh. The girl had pluck to urge him to continue fighting – but the risk was too great.

'Better do as I say, Callender,' persisted Cy Tambaugh. 'Throw your guns out and walk over here – or the girl gets ventilated!'

Stella tried to shout something, but it strangled in her throat as Tambaugh crooked his arm tighter about it.

'Use your head, Callender, throw down your guns and come over here,' yelled Tambaugh.

Will rose to his full height from behind the clutter of boxes and kegs at the front of the store, a dejected giant with a blood and sweat-crusted face. He tossed his Colts into the rutted, hoof-pocked street.

'OK, Tambaugh,' he husked. 'I'm comin'.'

# ELEVEN

A sneering grin spread over Cy Tambaugh's features as Callender came into the group of CT men, hands half-raised. The rancher's gunhands kept their weapons levelled at the capitulating Arizonan.

The cattle baron still held the girl in his grip. He was standing close to the hitch-rack outside the café, leering triumphantly at Will Callender.

'I've got you, Callender – alive, like I said I would!' he told him.

There was a sudden, distracting movement on the sidewalk outside Kurdia's café as a figure whipped through the door of that establishment.

'Take your hands off the girl!' came a terse voice from the plank-walk fronting the café. The CT men whirled about to face the voice.

Cy Tambaugh, still gripping Stella about the throat, snarled at the sight of Jake Kurdia standing in front of the café with a Colt levelled at Tambaugh. This was a new Kurdia, a Kurdia in whose eyes flared

murderous intent – a Kurdia far different from the
man who had long pandered to Tambaugh. The
mouth in his seamed and wrinkle-etched face was set
in a grim and determined line. The muzzle of the
Colt was directed unwaveringly at the man who held
his niece.

'Take your hands off her, Tambaugh,' he
repeated. 'No one paws my sister's girl that way!'

There was weighty silence for an instant while Cy
Tambaugh digested the novelty of the situation –
Jake Kurdia, who had toadied to Tambaugh's every
whim for so many years, turning on the cattle baron
with a gun.

'You're crazy,' sniggered Tambaugh. There was
much of that humour-lacking amusement he had
shown when Callender first faced him at the Palacio.
'You don't know what you're doing, Jake. You're
plumb crazy.' He still gripped Stella Rivers and his gun
was still forced into the small of her back. 'You could-
n't hit me without harming the girl,' he taunted. 'You
can't do a thing with that pop-gun, Jake.'

Kurdia stood his ground, the six-gun still levelled.

'You know me, Tambaugh. You know how I can
handle a gun. I figure I can take you in the head
from this close. Take your paws off Stella!' The
command was flat and cold and Jake Kurdia lifted
the six-gun dangerously.

There was no mistaking his intention, and
Tambaugh panicked into whipping his gun from
behind the captive's back and blazing a wild shot at
the man on the plank-walk. As he fired, the rancher

ducked down behind Stella so that he was completely shielded by her.

In that split instant, on the thin edge of triggering the Colt, Jake Kurdia realized the danger of his hitting Stella. His trigger-finger stilled in the very act of squeezing, and Tambaugh's wildly-thrown slug took him in the left shoulder. At this close range the force of the bullet sent him reeling backwards, his game leg crumpled under him and he twisted down to the boardwalk.

In that same split instant also, Will Callender used the distraction to act. He was standing among the CT men, some still mounted, others standing. In front of him was a cowpoke with a Colt .44 holstered at his hip. Callender made a grab for the gun the instant Tambaugh had fired. Even as his fingers closed over the butt of the weapon in the cow wrangler's gunbelt, a mounted CT man behind the Arizonan caught sight of the action from the corner of his eye. He leaned downwards and, with the big Smith & Wesson pistol that was in his hand, hit Callender over the bare head, pistol-whip fashion.

Will dropped down among the hooves and boots like a rag doll, senseless.

Tambaugh whirled about, throwing Stella from him; she instantly ran for the boardwalk where her uncle lay clutching his shoulder.

'What happened?' asked the rancher of the rider who had pistol-whipped Will.

'Tried to grab Slim's gun an' I slapped him over the cabeza with my gun,' came the laconic explanation.

'All right, somebody throw him over a cayuse. We're riding home so I can have a private talk with mister self-appointed town marshal here.'

'What about Kurdia?' someone queried.

'Leave him where he is,' retorted the rancher harshly. 'I guess that fool's had his enthusiasm dampened for good and all. Damned if he hasn't got himself tainted with some of his brother-in-law and niece's high ideals.'

They mounted up and rode northward for the CT ranges, the limp form of Will Callender draped over one of the wrangler's mounts. The sun was now blazing through the golden mist of an early south-western morning, and the dry wind blustering off the desert flats whipped the dust of their back-trail about the rutted street of Crimson Peak. They rode past the store where Callender had made his stand, with the body of the CT horseman the Arizonan had shot sprawled before it. They passed the marshal's office close to which the corpses of Clay Galliver, Mex Chavez and broken-necked Charlie Krantz stiffened in the morning air.

Stella Rivers, kneeling beside her injured uncle on the sidewalk fronting the restaurant and attending to his bullet-drilled shoulder, watched them go. She bit her lip and tried to fight back the tears that were welling in her eyes. Kurdia too was glowering after the CT bunch with hate-hardened eyes.

'Patch up my shoulder with something, girl,' he ordered between clenched teeth. 'I'm saddling up my horse!'

He struggled to his feet, wincing with pain.

'Uncle Jake, you can't ride after them!' the raven-haired girl protested.

'I can an' I must, Stella,' he replied firmly. There was a warmth in his tone that she had not heard for many years – since she had been a little girl, when he was a different Jake Kurdia. 'I can an' I must,' he repeated half to himself. 'It's got to do with a man provin' to himself that he's still a man.'

Although Cy Tambaugh had built his ranch-house on elegant lines, the architecture being borrowed from some Mexican hacienda, the remainder of the buildings of the CT ranch followed the usual pattern of those on any desert-range outfit. A scatter of adobe and wooden shacks and sheds circling a wide area holding the usual peeled pole corrals.

Into the yard of the ranch headquarters came Tambaugh and his riders. Callender, now recovered, was sitting slouched in the saddle of the horse of the man he had shot outside the store in Crimson Peak. The wound in his arm burned and his pistol-whipped head ached as though it had been trampled by a spooked steer. The CT rannihans, taking no chances on this wild gunhand from out of Arizona, kept weapons levelled on him and watched him with hard eyes narrowed against the brilliance of the now strong sun.

At the veranda of the stucco ranch-house the party came to a halt with the creak of leather.

'Lou, Slim, bring Callender into the house,'

ordered Cy Tambaugh, as the riders dismounted. 'I want a private chat with him.'

Two of the gunhawks, one tall, powerful and ape-faced, the other shorter and leaner, hoisted Will from the saddle roughly. With a detached portion of his mind he remembered two of the names he had forced out of Chet Conners that morning at the mine: Lou Killan and Slim Wheaton – two of the men who had been in on the killing of Bob. They prodded him with their revolvers up the steps of the veranda and into the house, followed by a triumphantly leering Tambaugh.

There was still a haze floating before Will's eyes. He was befuddled and a trifle unsteady on his long legs.

'In here,' ordered Cy Tambaugh, shoving a door open. Will found himself prodded into a wide living-room furnished with a sumptuousness rarely found west of the Pecos. One wall was ornamented with mounted weapons of earlier frontier days and a pair of record length horns from the head of some Texas beef-beast were hung on yet another. At the far end of the room a stained glass door window, giving on to the veranda, broke the blaze of the sun into a multitude of coloured shafts of light.

'Let our guest be seated,' murmured Tambaugh with a smirk. Ape-face shoved Callender forcibly into an armchair. The boss of the CT jerked his head towards the door, indicating dismissal, and the pair of gun-hung riders made to leave the room.

'Stick around outside,' Tambaugh ordered, 'until

I've finished my chat with Callender.'

The door clicked on the departing pair and Cy Tambaugh moved closer to Callender's chair. Under the neatly-cultivated moustache his mouth was drawn into a toothy sneer.

'Now, Callender,' he began in silky tones, 'you know what I want – news of Rosalind. I've wanted news of her for many years now – I want to know where she is—'

'Go to hell!' Will was gripping the arms of the chair, feeling as weak as a kitten, but presenting a defiant, blood-crusted face to the rancher. 'Go to hell, Tambaugh – you get to know about her when I get your story of the set-up in which my brother was killed!'

Tambaugh's eyes became hard as flint chips and narrowed dangerously. His voice took on a brittle edge. 'Why don't you quit acting up, Callender? I want word of Rosalind; she's the only person I care about in the whole world. Now, I'm not an unreasonable man—'

Again Will Callender cut the cattle baron short, this time with a laugh in which bitter hatred and scorn were mingled.

'Hah! You're not an unreasonable man! A man shot to shreds while sleeping in his cabin so his silver strike could be grabbed and branded with the CT iron; nesters crowded off their miserable little holdings so the CT's beeves could trample down their corn patches; political strings pulled so you got your fingers around a town and nearly everyone in it, settin' up a cowardly back-shooter an' a crazy kid to enforce your kind of law! I suppose none of those are the acts of an unreasonable man! I heard about you, Tambaugh, long before I came to New Mexico Territory. I heard about the bushwhackin's and the burnin's of your early days out here. Your dream of buildin' a cattle empire has damn' near come true; but you didn't build it – you gathered a bunch of slug-throwin' desert hawks around you an' plundered it!'

Tambaugh silenced the Arizonan's tirade by acting with a totally unexpected swiftness. He looped a bunched fist at Will's stubbled jaw, cracking a hard swipe across it. Callender was jerked back into the chair as though hit by a kicking mule. He gasped and made an effort to rise, but the rancher anticipated the action and drove a hefty poke into the seated man's stomach. Open-mouthed, with all the wind driven from him, Will curled in the chair, writhing.

'Get this, and get it good, Callender – I want one thing out of you and that's news of Rosalind's whereabouts. Nothing and nobody else but she has ever mattered to me, even though I haven't seen her in years. I'm getting that information out of you, and if my fists don't beat it out I'll call Wheaton and Killan in here to pistol-whip it out of you. Let's get started – where's Rosalind now?'

Callender snorted breathlessly and made another effort to pull himself out of the chair. Cy Tambaugh slapped the open palm of his hand across Callender's face.

'I'm not foolin' around with you for long, Callender,' he snarled. 'I'm givin' you Gentle Annie treatment compared with what my boys will hand out if I call 'em in here. I want to hear you talk and talk fast!'

'Shut your face, Tambaugh, or I'll drop you with no second thoughts about it,' snapped a voice off to his right.

The cattle baron of the CT spread whirled to see that the door window had swung open and a small, warp-legged figure was in the very act of stepping into the room. Blocking the blaze of the sun beyond the portal he made a defiant little picture.

Jake Kurdia with a Colt buckled at his waist and a big, wicked-looking Sharps buffalo carbine levelled at Cy Tambaugh.

Hatred blazed from the little café owner's eyes.

'Get your hands offa that boy, Tambaugh,' he rasped coldly, 'or I'll put a buffalo shell in your head that'll plaster the walls with your brains!'

Cy Tambaugh stood as though paralysed. He was whitefaced and bug-eyed. His jaw began to work up and down and did so several times before he got the words out:

'Kurdia! Now I know you're crazy!'

'Like I said – keep your face shut up tight,' Kurdia interposed. 'Don't try howlin' for your rannihans, or it's you for the Great Divide.'

The old café proprietor's slug-laced shoulder sagged stiffly, but he had no difficulty in holding up the heavy buffalo carbine levelled directly at the rancher, and Tambaugh could read the grim determination written on the wrinkled features of this man who had finally turned on him after dancing to his tune for so many years. He stood under the threat of that high-calibre weapon like a man rooted to the spot.

Jake Kurdia jerked his head towards the open door window.

'Snap out of it, son,' he urged Will, still gasping for breath in the chair. 'We have to get out of here, *muy pronto*! I wasn't seen sneakin' across the yard, but Tambaugh's hawks might swoop on us any minute.'

Callender, feeling as though he was at the slow recovery end of a three-day drunk, stood up on legs that might have been columns of jelly. Through the mist that still floated before his eyes he was aware of Tambaugh standing not a yard away. As though a devil possessed him and he was not responsible for his own actions he took a step forward and slammed his bunched knuckles into the rancher's mouth. He put every iota of his diminished strength into the blow, trying to hand Tambaugh a small payment on behalf of the many people he had wronged. Tambaugh reeled back like a drunkard, then crumpled to the floor, clutching his smashed mouth. Callender stood over him breathing hard.

'That's for my brother Bob an' ole Lone-Star Dobbins, an' the dozens of nesters you've bulldogged off the land!' he told Tambaugh. 'But it doesn't settle the account by a long way. The way I'm goin' to pay you off for Bob's death will be in bullets!'

'You'll pay nobody off,' spluttered Cy Tambaugh through blood-slobbering lips. 'You won't get off this outfit alive – either of you. You'll be as dead as your brother in twenty minutes' time. My boys'll gun you as soon as you try to run for it. Of course Bob Callender was killed on my orders. He struck silver around here and I run this territory – anything that's to be had around here is going to be had by me! I worked out the plan to have him hounded down as a killer and a robber and my boys carried it out – I'm telling you, Callender, because you'll be gunned down when you try to leave the CT.'

Will stood over the man on the floor, fists bundled into hard knots.

'You worked it all out, eh, Tambaugh,' he growled. The grey eyes in his blood and mud-plastered face were blazing like those of a madman. 'You had Clay Galliver ride into town that afternoon in my brother's clothing an' on his cayuse. He shot Henry Dirks, a clerk employed by you in your bank, an' robbed the place – you had one of your own employees murdered an' you robbed your own bank!'

Tambaugh raised himself on one elbow, brushing blood from his chin with the back of his hand. 'Dirks was a pawn in the game, Callender, just a fool bank clerk – I can afford to use men as pawns. Your brother was a fool. He'd been in town all that morning on a drunk to celebrate his big strike. He went back to his cabin to sleep it off. It was child's play for my boys to sneak out there and take his horse and clothing while he was snoring off the booze!'

Will Callender made a swift crouching action and swept the rancher's Colt from his belt. He stood over the prostrated man with those flinty eyes blazing.

'That's all I ever wanted to hear from you, Tambaugh,' he hissed. 'That's all I wanted to hear before I slam a slug into you!'

Jake Kurdia, standing with the Sharps carbine levelled at the downed rancher, thought for a panicky moment that the big Arizonan was about to blaze bullets into Tambaugh there and then.

'Come on, son,' he exclaimed, 'let's get the hell out of this.'

'I ought to do it now, Tambaugh,' breathed Callender, flourishing the Colt. 'From here on watch out for my bullets.'

'You won't ever do it, Callender. There are two gunnies on the other side of that door and the ranch is stiff with gunslingers. The two of you are going to sprawl dead in the dirt. I don't care about wanting you alive any more, Callender. I don't care about Rosalind any more – that's all in the past – all I care about now is seeing you two gunned down.'

With their weapons levelled at the man on the floor, Kurdia and Callender backed towards the open door window. Kurdia took a cautious glance into the yard. It was deserted, but the clang of cooking pots issued from the nearby galley. Across the yard more than a dozen unsaddled horses milled about in a large corral.

'Half the CT's *remuda* is corralled there,' whispered Kurdia as they backed close to the portal. 'My nag is tied down in a clump of brush out beyond the yard apiece – I had to Injun my way over here plumb cautious. If we can grab a cayuse apiece an' turn the rest of the horses loose they'll have a hard time chasin' us.'

Suddenly, Cy Tambaugh, still sprawled on the floor of the room, rolled himself across the floor so that the chair in which Will had recently been seated was between himself and the men at the open portal. As he rolled to cover, he yelled:

'Lou! Slim! Come in smoking!' at the top of his lungs.

Callender brushed Kurdia back through the open window with a sweep of his free arm and crouched, facing the door with the Colt he had taken from Tambaugh levelled.

'Run for those horses!' he ordered flatly. 'I'll take 'em!'

# TWELVE

Slim Wheaton was the first one to come barging into the room with a naked gun as Jake Kurdia made a bid for the horse corral across the yard. He came running in, flourishing his gun and looking quickly about him. Lou Killan was crowding on his heels, waving a Colt. Will Callender fired at Wheaton the instant the slightly-built rider made to throw the mouth of his revolver on him. The belch of Callender's gun stabbed a blaze of red flame towards Wheaton, and the bark of the gun slammed loudly through the confined space of the room.

Wheaton teetered forward and fell into the room on his face. Killan had more time to find Callender's position in the room and he came in firing through the swirl of acrid gunsmoke.

Callender ducked wildly as the ape-faced gunhand's shot shattered one of the open stained-glass windows, sending a shower of coloured shards of glass flying at his back. From a low crouch he fired twice through the curtain of gunsmoke. Lou Killan did an erratic, tangle-footed dance to one side, then he slumped hard against the wall close to the door. He slithered down the wall and lay still across the body of Slim Wheaton.

Will turned and hared out of the open window, running mechanically like a man in a dream and wondering where he was finding the energy to move so swiftly.

Behind him he could hear Cy Tambaugh mouthing something quite unintelligible at the top of his voice. He could see Kurdia running in his game-legged fashion and almost at the horse corral. With the tail of his eye he caught sight of flurried activity away to one side. A number of range-garbed figures, attracted by the shooting, were issuing from a bunkhouse building, waving weapons.

Callender ran onwards across the yard in the direction of the *remuda* corral. He could see Jake Kurdia, handicapped by his injured shoulder, trying to hold his heavy buffalo carbine and fumble open the gate of the corral at the same time.

A cacophany of yells sounded behind Callender, and somebody loosed a wild six-gun shot that went whining past his car like an angry hornet. He was still carrying the Colt he had taken from the boss of the CT spread, and he turned to loose an equally wild answering shot over his shoulder, almost as a reflex action.

He reached the horse corral panting, grunting and striving for breath, but somehow still with a whole hide.

The bunch of running CT wranglers were mere yards behind him. Jake Kurdia had the gate half opened. The horses were milling about in a broiling mass of hides, spooked by the yells and the firing.

'Get a couple of cayuses out,' said Kurdia with remarkable coolness. 'I'll hold these bunkhouse tramps off!'

He squatted down on one knee, soldier fashion, while Will began to drag the corral gate further open. Levelling the high-calibre weapon, Kurdia fired deliberately into the running bunch, now almost on top of them. The blast of the Sharps sent a flat clatter over the rangeland. There came a hoarse scream from the midst of the CT men, and a body plunked into the dust. The remainder of the pursuers, knowing that to face a buffalo-hunting gun at this range was tantamount to standing on the doorstep of hell when the portals were open, turned and scattered.

The firing of the powerful shell also had two other direct results. The first and major one was that it came when Will Callender had the horse corral gate almost fully open and the already scared animals were completely spooked by the loud, nearby explosion. The second, and minor, effect was that the kick of the weapon, which was usually fired from a stand spiked into the ground, threw Kurdia kicking on his back.

He was thrown clear of the rearing, whinnying mass of horseflesh that came through the corral gate in a cloud of hoof-churned dust.

On the further side of the gate Will Callender, realising that there was no controlling the mass of stampeding animals, dived away from the charging, crazed *remuda* and crouched at the base of a corral post.

He watched the horses go thundering across the yard, heading directly for the running CT men. Some of the men gained the safety of the ranch-house, but through the lingering dust pall two or three hoof-trampled bodies could be seen in the wake of the hazing animals. The spooked horses went pounding away across the yard in a wildly rearing body, finally scattering off across the rangeland with a plume of sun-touched dust to mark their passing.

Callender picked himself up and ran to where Kurdia sprawled spluttering in the dust. He helped the older man to his feet.

'There goes our chance of grabbin' a piece of horseflesh each,' he grumbled, squinting his wrinkle fringed eyes in the direction of the disappearing horses. 'We'll have to stand here an' fight,' he added solemnly.

'You say your horse is picketed close by,' Will retorted. 'Make a run for it an' ride home! I'll stick here – after all, this is my fight!'

'What!' snapped Kurdia, as though insulted. 'Leave you here? Nothin' doin', son. I've wanted a crack at Cy Tambaugh for years – but I got too damned lily-livered over the years. Now I'm beginnin' to feel like the old Jake Kurdia that used to be

– an' I'm lovin' it.' He fumbled in the pocket of his Eastern coat, produced another huge shell for the Sharps and began to reload the weapon.

'Then let's head for cover,' suggested Will, noting that Cy Tambaugh and a cluster of gun-packing gentry were massing on the veranda of the house on the far side of the yard. 'That barn over there is as good a place as any.'

They began to run through the curtain of dust left lingering in the back-trail of the maddened horses, heading for a high barn away to their right. They heard Cy Tambaugh's voice yell:

'There they go – gun 'em!'

The guns of Tambaugh and his crowd began to blast as Will and Kurdia made the barn door which faced the ranch-house. Bullets sputtered up dry spouts of dust at their heels as they threw themselves into the mouth of the door and flattened to the floor. Callender fired from the gloom of the barn's interior, dropping one of the CT gunhands over the rail of the veranda like a marionette whose strings had been cut. He fired again and again until the Colt in his hand clicked emptily. He sought the cover of some hay bales to reload from the cartridge loops at his belt. Kurdia was blasting away with his own six-shooter, the men on the veranda were scattering for whatever cover they could find while answering with ragged shots.

Will came out from behind the bales with a newly-charged gun, blasting bullets at the CT wranglers. Kurdia was crouching to one side of the barn door with a flaming Colt and a grinning face. Bullets whanged and screamed about the barn, sending slivers of wood ripping from the sun-dried structure. A number of CT gunmen lay sprawled on the veranda of the house; Cy Tambaugh was nowhere to be seen.

Most of the attack now came from behind the adobe-bricked buildings dotted about the wide yard, the CT gunnies having retreated to them in preference to the too-exposed veranda.

Kurdia cast his empty Colt to one side, squatted down into a new position with the buffalo gun and dropped a too bold CT man who ventured from behind a 'dobe wall with a levelled Winchester into a shell-shattered, lifeless heap. Kurdia picked himself up from where the kick of the powerful weapon had thrown him and grinned at Will, who was lying on his stomach on the floor of the barn triggering shots out into the yard.

'I usta be a buffler hunter in the plains country before I drifted West,' Kurdia said. 'There was a time when I could handle this cannon as easy as if she was a babe in arms – still, I ain't doin' so badly for a *hombre* with a shot-up wing.'

He began to thumb another shell into the weapon while Will took a shot at the top of a hat protruding over a water barrel near the cook's galley. Kurdia came forward to crouch at the door, covering the yard with the carbine while Callender replenished the cylinders of both his own and his companion's six-gun.

From outside the slam of guns came barking out

a fresh burst of hot lead. Callender ducked to one side of the door as bullets riddled the jamb close to his head.

He triggered an answer in hot lead while Jake Kurdia sent yet another high-calibre shell whining across the yard, firing at no one in particular, but knowing that no fighter using a six-gun would care to face 30-30 shells. Kurdia knew that his high-powered weapon would strike terror into the opposition and he delighted in using it.

That loud-barking weapon, sending its devastating charges screaming across the yard of the CT outfit was having a strong psychological effect. The CT gunnies were now keeping very much under cover and sending only wild shots in the direction of the barn in which the two men were making their stand.

'By grab, it's a long time since I was in a bullet banquet,' grinned Kurdia. 'The last exchange of lead I was in, I regret to say, was a little fracas in which CT rannihans crowded a bunch of wire-fence homesteaders off the range, so Tambaugh could grab the miserable strip of land they'd settled on.' A more sober note settled into his voice. 'I ain't got much use for fences on the open range, any more than any other cowman has, but I'm sure ashamed of myself for the bit I played in runnin' those nesters off that day – an' a good many more nesters on other days. Maybe I can square myself for all that right now – in a sort of re-baptism of fire.' As though to emphasize his point he blasted his Colt at a sombrero-topped head that came peering gingerly around the wall of an adobe shed.

Kurdia watched the face disappear abruptly behind the wall, open-mouthed and drilled between the eyes.

'You're a good man with a gun,' observed Callender, slamming a couple out across the sun-blasted yard.

'I don't reckon I lost my touch any. I used to run around the plains with a pretty wild crowd when I was a youngster – picked up a deal of gun-savvy up in Wyoming an' Dakota. That's the territory where a man has to be slick with his trigger. If he ain't runnin' up agin bad Injuns he's up agin bad whites. There's no tellin' which is worse!'

The men in the barn fell silent for a few seconds, both conscious that an unusual tranquillity had settled on the headquarters of the CT.

'Gone awful quiet all of a sudden,' murmured the restaurant owner from Crimson Peak. 'D'you figure those rats are runnin' out? Ain't many guys who'll face a Sharps gun.'

'Can't say,' replied Callender, wriggling forward along the floor of the barn to take a look outside.

The CT gunmen seemed to be well entrenched in their various points of cover. No one showed himself and no shots were fired. 'A Sharps buffalo carbine can throw a powerful scare into any man. We seem to have split Tambaugh's crowd into several little parcels, but I didn't see anybody hightailin'—' Callender broke off, sniffing something that mingled ominously with the cordite stench of the drifting gunsmoke.

Both he and his companion twisted their heads about at the noise of an ominous crackling, sounding from the rear of the barn.

A black wisp of smoke drifted from out of the gloom of the barn.

'Fire!' snorted Kurdia. 'So that's it! Someone sneaked around the back of the place and put a light to it – this place will burn like tinder too.'

Will Callender set his mouth in a grim line. At the rear of the barn where the wall met the ground a thick, black billow of smoke was seeping upwards and the gloom was relieved by the flicker of ever-growing flames.

'It's blazin' plenty,' growled Will. 'I figure Tambaugh and his crowd are just lyin' low waitin' for us to be smoked out – then they'll blast us down.'

At their backs the flames were increasing and the smoke filled the barn. Several bales of hay and straw were now alight. Callender clutched Kurdia's sleeve urgently.

'Listen, Kurdia,' he began. 'We don't stand a Chinaman's chance with this place blazin' the way it is. It's stay here an' roast or run out into their gunfire! I guess I'll call Tambaugh's hand an' see if he'll gun it out with me, man to man. It'll give you a chance to get out of here an' me a chance of settlin' what's between us.'

'It won't work,' Kurdia said. 'Tambaugh's yellow as a snake's belly.'

Will Callender made no answer. He wriggled forward in the dust until he was close to the door through which acrid smoke was now belching in heavy palls. He bellowed into the yard:

'Hey, Tambaugh, wherever you are! There's no point in all this war-makin'! Come out with a Colt an' we'll smoke it out – just you an' me!'

There was no reply, but through the drifts of swirling smoke, he saw one or two inquisitive faces peering from cover.

'Come on out an' fight, Tambaugh!' yelled Will at the top of his lungs. 'You an' me, Tambaugh – man to man!'

There was still no reply to the Arizonan's challenge. He turned to psychological tactics:

'You yellow, Tambaugh?' he roared across the yard. 'I guess it's great by you to have these *hombres* doin' your gunnin' for you so you can skulk away while they have the option on a buffalo shell in the brain! How about comin' out an' facin' me?'

No reply. Behind him the flames licked higher around the barn and the smoke billowed high. Jake Kurdia crawled through the thick haze of smoke and squatted close to the blazing building, covering the silent ranch-yard with the Sharps.

Will continued his challenge: 'Like I just said, Tambaugh – you're yellow! You wouldn't face me on the street in town an' you won't face me now – so long as you can get these mutts to pull their triggers for you! Come out an' face me – we'll get to squarin' our debts personal.' Callender knew that if he could keep up this line of challenge long enough he might succeed in causing the CT gunhands to lose faith in their employer.

'Let's get down to it, Tambaugh – are you comin' out to fight, or do I have to get around to callin' you insultin' names to bring you out?'

There was no reply for a moment, then there was a movement from behind an adobe barn. Tambaugh was coming out – being pushed out to face the Arizonan by one of his gunhands. Callender felt a surge of jubilance rush through him as he went striding, long-legged and half crouched out of the smoke.

It had worked! His shouting had set the CT gunmen to asking themselves why they should risk their necks in fighting Tambaugh's battles when the rancher was too scared to face his enemy and smoke their differences out. They were forcing Cy Tambaugh out from behind the cover of the adobe-bricked barn.

From that direction a raucous voice bawled: 'He's comin', Callender, carryin' a six-gun! He faces you – or we back-shoot him our own selves.'

From out of the swirling, dense smoke Will advanced with the forward leaning, cat-footing approach of the gunfighter. In the background Jake Kurdia sat with the buffalo gun levelled, watching warily for treachery. Cy Tambaugh came into the open hesitantly, carrying a Colt and watching the gaunt, gun-carrying figure silhouetted against the blaze of the barn with apprehension. Both men advanced in a silence broken only by the crackling of the tinder-dry barn, now a vast sheet of flame.

Then Tambaugh proved amazingly quick. With the speed of a striking rattler he threw the barrel of his gun in Callender's direction and fired.

Will ducked and threw himself to one side, cursing the fact that his reactions seemed to be hopelessly slowed down. Cy Tambaugh's slug went whanging over his head as he felt his ankle twist and he went sprawling down into the sun-painted dust. He hit the ground heavily on his side and, rolling to gather himself up, had a madly whirling view of Tambaugh dancing dervish fashion to position himself for taking an easy and languid shot at him as he sprawled in the dirt.

He rolled frenziedly to find free movement for his gun hand, and somehow got the Colt levelled from his difficult firing position and blasted a red slash of muzzle-fire up at the rancher before he could fire.

Cy Tambaugh skipped back on his heels, head down on his chest. He fired while in the very act of falling backwards, to lie spreadeagled and still, but the bullet merely ploughed a furrow and sent dry dust pluming a yard from Callender's position.

Will gathered himself up quickly and stood with gun levelled, trying to watch all the points which offered cover for the CT men at once. Silently Jake Kurdia appeared at his back, holding the buffalo gun menacingly.

From behind barns and shacks came CT gunnies, converging cautiously upon the point in the centre of the yard where the two stood prepared for action.

One of them, a tall, black-garbed and intelligent-looking man who looked as though he might once have been anything from a professional gambler to a frontier preacher, advanced a little closer than the rest. Slowly, as though making a symbol of the action, he placed the big Navy Colt he carried into the low-slung holster at his right thigh.

'That's the end, *amigo*,' he said to Callender in smooth and cultured tones. 'No more fight for us. Tambaugh's dead, your quarrel's settled and we have nothing against you. You know our brand, Callender, the border breed. We'll throw slugs for a man and take a chance on living to collect the big money he pays for our services – but when he's dead there's no one left to remunerate us, so we check out. I disagree with Shakespeare, *amigo*, the evil that men do dies with them, and my companions agree. So we'll saddle up and ride elsewhere, holding no hard feelings against you and your friend.'

Will stood befuddled and still clutching his Colt, wondering whether this suave, classic-quoting talk was a lead-up to treachery.

'It's not settled!' He rapped out the words harshly while his half-dazed mind was riffling through the names Chet Conners had given him at the mine on Silica Ridge – the names of the men who had been at the killing of his brother that he had filed away in his mind with his precise lawman's method. 'It's not settled – I want two more men, two who were in on the Silica Ridge killing – Ace Pocock and Rudy Steptoe!'

The black-clad gunslinger smiled smoothly.

'You'll have to take my word for it, Callender, but they're both dead – Pocock's over there on the veranda and what's left of Steptoe, after the stampeding *remuda* trampled him, is yonder in the dirt. None of the rest of us were in on that killing, so your account's squared.'

Callender and Kurdia still stood their ground, holding their weapons, wary and suspicious. But the CT gunmen were putting up their guns, turning their backs and walking away. They moved without a glance at Tambaugh lying in the dust.

Behind Callender and the restaurant owner the flame eaten shell of the burning barn fell inwards in a roaring rush of sparks. It was like a full stop to an episode.

Then both men whirled at a painful croaking sound:

'Callender!'

They saw that Cy Tambaugh was still alive and was making his way towards them, pulling himself slowly through the dust.

Tambaugh was coming, crawling!

# THIRTEEN

There was no triumph in Will Callender because Cy Tambaugh was now clawing urgently at his legs, and yet there was sympathy for the dying man in him. Tambaugh had dragged himself gunless through the dust of the smoke-shrouded yard of the CT ranch. Blood bubbled from his lips and the mark of death was stamped plainly on his features.

Jake Kurdia watched the scene without emotion. Most of the gunhands had now drifted away and were saddling up their mounts at the stables flanking the ranch-house. For them an episode in their lives as gun-for-hire drifters had closed. They would ride on elsewhere and eventually sell their guns into somebody else's fight somewhere along the bullet-bitten border.

Callender bent his lean body, squatting beside the dying rancher. Tambaugh's voice was only a croaking whisper:

'Callender, I want to know about her! Rosalind – where is she?'

'Dead,' said Will. The word was flat, cold, entirely without feeling. 'In the Chicago typhoid epidemic nine years ago.'

'Dead!' husked the white-faced, dying man unbelievingly. 'Rosalind dead all these years?'

'She was one of many,' replied Will coldly and detachedly. 'A lot of people died at that time.'

Tambaugh was sinking fast, his body quivering and his eyes half-closed. Will cradled the dying man's head in his arms. An inquiring portion of his brain asked why he was doing so, and the answer was that maybe he was doing it for Rosalind's sake.

'She was everything to me,' said Tambaugh with difficulty. He waved a weak arm at the ranch buildings and the sweep of the wide land around them. 'All this – I started it for her sake – at first – then it got bigger – I got—' he struggled against a cough that racked his body. Callender finished the sentence:

'You got more powerful and greedy,' he said icily. 'You found you could hire guns and run folk off land you wanted by murder an' butchery an' fire. Your loved ones deserted you an' power, plunder, money an' the buildin' of a range empire was all you cared about.'

Tambaugh's eyes were closed, his breath coming in spasmodic wheezes.

'And Rosalind – I always cared about Rosalind – through all the years of separation. Was she anything to you, Callender?'

'I loved her,' said Will, 'in a way.'

Tambaugh tried to make a reply, but his head jerked back in an uncontrollable shudder and a rattle started in his throat. Then his head flopped down on to his chest.

'Let's go home,' Kurdia said.

'We'll bury him first,' Callender answered. And a voice in his mind added: 'For Rosalind's sake.'

They came into Crimson Peak in the blaze of afternoon, Kurdia riding his old nag and Callender a bloodied and punished figure on the saddleless back of one of the scared-off CT horses he had managed to catch.

Kurdia had talked plenty on the ride from the CT. 'Like I said back there, it's been a kind of re-baptism of fire,' he had opined. 'I proved to myself I was still a man. I developed into a number of kinds of a louse over the years, Callender. When I got crippled in that steer-breaking accident I guess I got soured plenty. I took it out on my sister's girl, to my eternal shame. I guess I deserved far worse than that draggin' over the counter you gave me when you first came to Crimson Peak. I bawled at Stella plenty and worked her plumb hard. But I was always fond of the girl in my own way. Seein' Tambaugh grab her the way he did was too much.'

'Forget it,' advised Will.

'That was the last straw,' went on Kurdia, heedless of the other's remarks. 'After he grabbed Stella and dragged her from the café – dragged her from her very bed, the polecat – I quit bein' a Tambaugh bootlicker an' got back to bein' what I was years ago – nobody's man but my own. Stella dressed the slug wound in my shoulder an' I grabbed my ole buffler huntin' carbine an' rode after the CT crowd at a sensible distance.'

'Forget it, Jake,' repeated Will. 'It's all in the past now.'

Stella Rivers met them as they entered the deserted café. Her gently-moulded oval features showed signs of much strain.

'Uncle Jake – Will!' she cried. 'I've been half crazy with worry – what happened?'

'Tambaugh is dead, my girl, that's the main thing that happened,' grinned Kurdia jubilantly. 'The days of the CT are over an' men an' women in these parts can call their souls their own!' The café owner bowlegged into the living quarters of the café. 'I'm gonna get the bathtub filled with hot water so we can each have a bath – then we'll get ourselves some sleep,' he announced. He went his way – singing in a cracked voice.

Stella smiled wanly at the Arizonan. 'I haven't seen Uncle Jake in that mood since I was very small,' said she.

'He's found himself again, Stella. To use his own words, he's been re-baptised by fire – he's all man, your uncle!'

The girl reached up and touched the tin star still on his vest. He had put it there as a gesture of defiance after running Tambaugh's so-called marshal out of town, and had completely forgotten about it.

'Are you staying on in town, marshal?' she asked. He unfastened the star and laid it on the counter.

'No, I guess the folk of Crimson Peak can elect themselves a new town marshal all correct an' legal – the way it should be done.'

'Will you go back to the Arizona Rangers?'

'I'm undecided – depends on a certain step I have to take – but I always wanted to run a horse ranch. I've saved enough capital an' I have my eye on some land up Holbrook way. I figure it would be fine to settle down to that kind of life.'

'Maybe you'll take a wife,' said the girl. 'I heard some of Tambaugh's men say something about someone called Rosalind – you used that name on some occasion – it meant something to Tambaugh – if she's the girl you're going to marry, I hope you'll be very happy!' The words came quick and blurted as she turned her head away quickly, tears in her eyes.

'Rosalind?' echoed Will, becoming deadly serious. 'Now see here, Rosalind's dead an' has been for nine years. If you want to know who she was and why I used her name when facing Tambaugh, I'll tell you – then you can call me all names you know for dragging her into this fight of mine with Tambaugh. I wasn't always what I am now, Stella, despite my dress an' way of talkin'. There was a time when I studied medicine in Chicago – my folks died an' I gave up my studies, partly because I wasn't cut out for a doctor and partly because I wanted to keep my young brother, Bob, at his engineering studies –

that's how I came to join the Arizona Rangers. While I was in Chicago I met two people from the South-West, a mother an' daughter. The girl was my own age. She was lovely and gentle and I thought I loved her, but I know now it was only pity. You see, she'd been blind from birth.'

Will paused and swallowed hard as the memories of those other days came crowding on him.

'I found out things about the girl, Rosalind, and her mother. They were living in Chicago only temporarily, then moving somewhere further east. The mother had taken the girl away from her father, a rancher in New Mexico, when a child, because he was developin' into something seen all too often in the West – a land-grabber, gettin' deeper an' deeper into the mire of murder and plunderin'. The mother had brought her child away from all this. They used her maiden name, but the family was—'

'Tambaugh!' guessed Stella Rivers.

Will nodded.

'I'm no philosopher, Stella, I don't know what makes a man good or bad. Tambaugh told me before he died that he started the CT empire for Rosalind's sake. Maybe he did. He might have once been just a hard strivin' man out to build somethin' for his wife an' his handicapped daughter; then he got too ambitious, too graspin', an' became some-thin' else again. Anyway, his wife left him to his land-grabbin' an' took their baby daughter with her. Rosalind died in an epidemic an' I came back to the South-West. When I heard about the killin' of my brother I made investigations an' heard it had happened in a part of New Mexico where a man named Tambaugh ruled the roost. I knew who I was up against an' I used the line that I knew of Rosalind's whereabouts just to help even the odds in my favour. I knew Tambaugh would not be so quick to kill me if I said I knew somethin' of his long-lost daughter. Now, you can call it mean an' cheap an' any other name you wish!'

Stella laid a hand on his arm.

'I don't call it anything of the sort, Will. You had every right to use any weapon you could against Tambaugh's force.'

They fell silent for an instant, then she asked: 'You said something about having to take a certain step a while back, what is that step?'

'To ask you to marry me!' he blurted.

Stella tried to answer through the tears of happiness misting her eyes, but he swept her into his arms and kissed her.

Outside a heavy pall seemed to have been lifted off Crimson Peak; even the tyrant sun of the desert edge had taken on a milder glow and there was something fresh in the air – like the promise of happiness for young people in love.